A Soldier

of the

Revolution

Also by Ward Just

A Soldier

of the

Revolution

WARD JUST

PublicAffairs   New York

To Walter Pincus & Frank Wisner

Book design by Mark McGarry, Texas Type & Book Works
Set in Dante

Library of Congress Cataloging-in-Publication data
Just, Ward S.
A soldier of the revolution / Ward Just.—1st PublicAffairs ed.
p. cm.
ISBN 1–58648–097–9 (pbk)
1. Corporations, American—Employees—Fiction. 2. Americans—
South America—Fiction. 3. Political violence—Fiction. 4. South
America—Fiction. 5. Insurgency—Fiction. I. Title.
PS3560.U75 S65 2002   813'.54—dc 21   2001060387

FIRST PUBLICAFFAIRS EDITION 2002
10 9 8 7 6 5 4 3 2 1

Chapter One

THE ROAD BEGAN at the church. It edged up the slope of one high hill, then down to a valley and the peak of another hill and out and down again across one stream and another, and so on a hundred times to the border. The country was plateau, a region of black earth and rocks and huts and animals and beyond them mountains in mist. The summits of the mountains were dim on the horizon, and often invisible altogether; on the far side, twenty-one thousand feet down, was the jungle.

The road was never more than ten feet wide, a collection of ruts and pits tilting here and there generally east into the interior. From nowhere to nowhere, a nonroad to nonplaces, as the priests described it; up a hill, down a valley, the way out. The church where the road began dominated Acopara, the sullen and uninviting market town of the district. The church and its window were elegant by contrast, and the radio tower a modern miracle. Up the slopes of the hill were the houses, white and dry as bones in the sun, invisible unless you knew they were there, difficult to distinguish in the beginning. They became familiar with time, seen every day from the road or from the plaza in front of the church. The houses ringed the town to the east and north as seats in an amphitheater, as much a part of the mountain as the rocks and the short stubble scrub, the high sky, and the patches of light green in the valleys. The atmosphere was light at twelve thousand feet, a wonderful light blue hinged always by luminous cirrus clouds, at sunset dazzling, a color so light and fine that it seemed given in compensation for the other things. Instead of food and heat, the people had sunrise and sunset.

In the mornings, the sun pierced the thin air, burning everything it touched except the land. The altitude cooled the atmosphere and most evenings were so clear that by starlight you could see the wrinkles in a man's hand. But the air was cold, and when it rained it was a torrent. On the high plain the danger was the wind, that and the lightning and hail the size of small melons. The people feared the cold, the wind and the rain, the lightning and the hail, as natural and permanent circumstances. Not often seen in the countryside, the people kept out of sight, either in the houses or in the gardens back of the houses, or further out, into the hills or the plateau, tending to the animals or to each other. They were the occupants of the land, the people and the animals, but they were not visible. On bad days, they remained in their huts, one pressed against the other for warmth, intimate to survive the circumstances. The people who lived nearby came frequently to town, to sell goods and do the marketing. It was four hours by foot, two by mule, an hour by jeep to run a distance of ten miles, here to there in Acopara district. Distance on the plain was measured in time, which is to say measured in difficulty. The Indians hustled, moved as if all appointments were urgent, scuttled along the sides of the road like crabs, darting to the ditch at the noise of an approaching car, heads bent, bouncing the bundle of sticks or produce fastened to their backs. The women were heavy, heavy bellied and heavy faced; to a foreigner's eye, misshapen from struggle. The men were nondescript, dark-faced, dark-clothed, dark of spirit. Seeking strength, does a people cast its face to the sun or to the earth? On the high plain, the Indians gazed resolutely down, expecting their fortunes to be read from the black earth and the rocks, and the cold wind that swept over them like the tide.

One mile was five for an Indian and ten or fifteen for a European or North American, or for anyone from outside. Foreigners moved about with economy because of the height, twelve thousand feet in the town and fifteen and sixteen thousand feet forty miles out of it. But foreigners seldom ventured outside Acopara. The height controlled movement as definitely as a glacier or a canyon. Those who lived on the plain for any length of time found their lungs expanded. It was a healthy place for a European or a North American, a spa; germs and viruses did not thrive in the climate. Foreigners who came to stay needed to decompress, exactly as if they had ascended to the surface from the bottom of the sea. In some, the thinness of the air caused disorientation. Others relaxed, shunned physical exercise; took it, as Father Deshais said, as it came.

Reardon was up at eight in the morning and heard the bells. His room was back of the church, one of many rooms down a long corridor in a heavy, gloomy building, once fine, now in dishabille.

Brother Irwin was on one side, Father Francis on the other. Father Thomas was across the hall, in the "suite." Reardon heard Peter Francis get up an hour before, rustle around clumsily and leave, but the other two were still sleeping. Reardon felt disinclined to move, so he stood in the middle of the room, fully dressed, his arms folded, staring out the window into the street. He saw himself in profile from the corner of his eye, aslant in the mirror above the bureau, framed as a portrait. How long could a man stand still, do nothing, not move a nerve or twitch? Not long, not long at all. Reardon walked to the window and looked out. He saw a stray dog, a few people, a minor official in the town whom he knew; Gutierrez, the physician, was waddling toward the church. Could a man stand immobile for five hours? Fix his sight on a spot in the middle distance and not move at all, erase his mind of thought, become a statue? Not likely. Well, he would have to move.

He collected his money and his watch from the bureau, stuffed the bills in his pocket, and wrapped the watch around his wrist. The day fitted the mood: dark, melancholy. Brother Bicker was departing, an involuntary casualty, a victim of the height. Reardon turned and walked out, leaving the door ajar, and moved down the corridor to Bicker's room. He knocked softly and heard a noise, but no answer.

"Bicker!"

"A moment," a muffled voice said.

"It's Reardon."

"One minute."

Reardon leaned against the door jamb, his arms folded, and waited. The clang of the bells filled the house.

"One hour to train time, Bicker. And it will take us thirty minutes to get there through the streets, and I have got to get gas."

"The Lord will provide," Bicker said.

"Bullshit," said Reardon.

The door opened, and Bicker motioned him inside. The room was in violent upheaval. Bits of clothing were strewn about the floor and hung from the bureau. Two opened suitcases were on the unmade bed, and there was Bicker in his shorts, grinning, holding a silver picture frame in one hand and a shoe tree in the other.

"Have a beer."

"Great, Bicker. That's what's needed now."

"On the window sill."

"Yeah, but there isn't much time," Reardon said, looking at the debris, wondering where all of it came from. "You don't want to miss the train. Think of the problems if you miss the train."

Bicker handed Reardon an unopened bottle of beer, the local brand, ice-cold to the touch. "First things first," he said.

Reardon was watching him closely, but Bicker seemed no more manic than usual. He had to get packed, collected, out of there. Reardon began stuffing clothing into the suitcase, while Bicker stood looking out the window, still holding the picture frame and the shoe tree. He tucked the shoe tree under his arm when he took a sip of beer from the bottle on the window sill. He was humming softly to himself, a *Te Deum*.

"Packed, Bicker. Time to get packed."

"All right, all right!"

"How do you feel?"

"Lousy and happy. Happy-lousy."

He put down the beer and the picture frame and went absent-mindedly to the closet. There he selected his wardrobe for the day, pulling out sleeves and trouser legs from the mass inside, inspecting the cloth carefully, taking the threads between thumb and forefinger, pursing his lips. Bicker was heavy, a large man, balding on top, slouched and out of shape, messy when he walked. He pulled from the closet grey flannel trousers and a checked flannel shirt and his white tennis hat. It was what he always wore.

Reardon jammed things into Bicker's bags.

"Have to say good-bye to Deshais," Bicker said.

"Deshais's saying mass."

"I'll wave from the transept."

"Oh, Deshais will love that."

"A red flag, Reardon. How's that?"

"Fine, Bicker."

Bicker was dressed, and the bags packed, in fifteen minutes.

"What about the boxes?" Reardon pointed to half a dozen whisky cartons in the corner of the room. Bicker nodded, and crooked his finger; he took Reardon by the arm, and brought him over to the boxes.

"These are them," Bicker said.

"What?"

"The holy cards, Reardon."

"Oh."

"There will be no one to distribute them when I am gone."

"Right."

"So you must do that."

"Right."

"I'm serious, Reardon. This is very important."

"I know."

"I am leaving them in your charge."

"Okay, Bicker."

"You will take over from me."

"Fine."

"So now they are yours. I will leave them here. You can get them any time."

"Come on, Bicker. It's time to go."

Wrestling the heavy bags, Reardon and Bicker staggered down the corridor. They waved hello to the mestizo cook who was making bacon and pancakes, whistling tunelessly in the empty kitchen. Bicker dropped his bag to shake hands and wish luck to the cook. The cook wanted to help with the bags, but Bicker waved him away; no, no, you must *cook*. The two of them went out the alley to the parking lot and Reardon's jeep. The jeep belonged to the mission and was technically assigned to Deshais; but Deshais did not drive and had nowhere to go, so Reardon leased it from him, and used it in his rounds.

They put the bags in the back, and Bicker turned and said he would meet Reardon in the plaza.

"No time, Bicker," Reardon said.

"I've got to say good-bye to Deshais."

"Oh, no, Bicker."

"Yep," Bicker said, and trotted back into the building. It was the rear entrance to the mission. The church was reached by a series of interlocking passageways. Reardon, smiling, watched him go. He would probably do what he said he would do, wave a red flag from the transept. And Deshais would avert his eyes, and go straight to the breviary. Bicker, Brother Geoffrey Justin Bicker, gentle, sweet-tempered, and mad as a hatter. In a moment he was back.

"Wait!" he said. "Jesus Christ."

"What?"

"I left my crucifix on the wall. Wait a minute."

Reardon was still laughing when Bicker returned, carrying the crucifix. "Here," he said. "Stuff it into one of the bags. I'll meet you at the plaza."

Reardon backed the jeep out of the lot, turned, and cautiously poked it into the street amid the hurrying people. He lightly tapped the horn, and the people ignored him; then he pressed it with the heel of his hand and eased out of the driveway. Reardon moved the jeep into the street, driving toward the Plaza de Armas along the yellow brick sides of the church. The people paid him no mind, and he accelerated slowly, never moving faster than the people. In the front of the church in the plaza the beggars were all in place: three men and four women today, all blind, one sawing a tune on a violin, another selling knitted hats, a third standing stiffly, as if that was all that should be necessary to earn a reward from passers-by. The others had so arranged themselves on the sidewalk to force communicants bound for mass to confront them first, an obstacle course, a minefield of misery. Gutierrez, fresh from a coffee at the café, head down and moving swiftly, got by safely as he did most mornings. But a few people stopped and pulled coins from their pockets. The profits were shared after the service, which all the poor naturally attended, tithing one per cent of the morning's receipts. Pins of candlelight shown from inside the church, and as Reardon passed he heard singing; that, and the shuffling of feet.

He stopped the jeep and saw Bicker emerge and give a bill to each of the seven beggars. He spoke a few words to each beggar as he handed them the bills. Then Reardon looked closely and saw they were not bills at all, but holy cards. He was giving holy cards to the beggars, and the beggars knew it. They were not smiling, and there was only one *gracias* from the seven of them, and that given grudgingly. Deshais would no doubt get the holy cards in the collection plate.

"Okay," Bicker said, climbing into the jeep. "Let's go." He slumped down in the front seat, his knees up against the dashboard, feet dangling.

"You made a big hit with the *pobres,* Bicker."

"Sure," he said.

"A regular orgy of gratitude."

Bicker didn't reply.

Reardon turned at the far end of the plaza, down a narrow street whose irregular stones tilted the jeep. Now there were a few stragglers, most of them women who hurried with their heads bent, one or two children in tow, heading for church. They were short, heavy-chested people, dressed in black, and they walked with a stoop. Along the sides of the road, some stood staring at the pavement. The small shops were opening, their owners standing in doorways looking about, rubbing their hands, looking forward to business, keeping an eye out for chiselers, panhandlers, and children; for thieves. Some of them waved at the jeep, and Reardon returned the waves, moving his lips as he did, soundlessly, keeping his mind on the road, *good morning, good morning,* then passing on to the wide road split in the middle by railroad tracks, and beyond it the low plain, the hills, and the mountains. He stopped at the edge of town to fill the car with gas.

—*"Cómo está?"*

—*"Bien, Señor Reardon. Bien."*

Well, always well. The people were always getting on. He and Bicker sat in the front without speaking, and watched the Indians bartering in the market place across the road. The dealer in coca was doing excellent business, as always. The Indians were selling skins and sweaters and vegetables. A small knot of them was gathered around two tourists, self-conscious Americans trying to bargain in the spirit of the country. An occasional tourist appeared in Acopara, due mainly to the eccentric railroad schedules, which required an overnight stay on the way to the celebrated ruins near the border. The tourists stayed for a night, then left. Reardon watched the bargaining for a moment, amused at the expressions of the Indians, who were wary and suspicious of the Nikons round the necks of the visitors. They despised having their pictures taken, believing their souls were captured in the small black box. It was good reason for caution if you were an Indian, since the black boxes were everywhere and usually focused and clicking. Reardon thanked and paid the gas station attendant. Bicker gave him a holy card, and they drove off.

"The railroad station," Reardon said.

"Sure," Bicker mumbled.

He had arrived six weeks before, a farmer in upstate New York before becoming a laybrother in the service of God. It was Bicker's first mission, a replacement for an elderly brother stricken with hepatitis and ordered home. Bicker settled in, satisfied, untroubled, in the first weeks performing the duties of a conscientious laybrother, monitoring the irrigation project, visiting the model farm each day, organizing charities. At first he accompanied Reardon on his rounds, to get the feel of the country, he said, a sense of the people. He went with Reardon twice into the countryside, and then he didn't go. He told Reardon later that the plain stunned him, its emptiness appalling and finally terrifying, the Indians a riddle. In his third week, he spent much of his time in the church, at prayer. Then he discovered the boxes of holy cards, tucked away in the basement of the church. They had been ordered years ago by O'Hara, a priest now gone. The new, modern-minded men did not want them, so the holy cards had stayed packed up in the basement until the day Bicker discovered them.

The others thought it a mordant joke, old-fashioned holy cards from a liberal brother like Bicker. But Reardon did not. Reardon was the only one to take him seriously, and only partly out of friendship.

Bicker announced that the holy cards were a grace, and the only grace that there was on the high plain. He took them with him wherever he went. At Deshais's late at night, he spoke enigmatically of the Indians, people who lived alone at great heights. At length he formulated a scheme for printing holy cards at Acopara. It began playfully, a combination of the spiritual and the economic. Increase employment, he said, make the printing plant inefficient, overstaff it with workers to manufacture a variety of cards to appeal to every Indian taste. Hire Indian artists. He thought that Reardon's foundation could finance the project.

—C'mon Reardon, cough up a few thousand dollars. We'll build the plant right here, employ hundreds.

—Wonderful, Bicker. I know I can sell it to the board. The Harris Foundation Holy Card Complex.

—Tell you what, Reardon. I will offer a mass said *in perpetuity.* For you and yours. How's that?

—Great. What about Harris?

—Them too.

The other duties forgotten, Bicker vowed to touch every Indian on the plain, and commenced to devote himself entirely to the holy cards, setting out early in the morning and driving great distances. Then one day he distributed three hundred cards, a week's supply; it took him twelve hours to do it. He called it the world's record, and defied anyone to break it. He distributed that day like a dervish, driving faster than anyone had a right to drive on the road, breaking routine to strike straight across the plateau where he knew of a family of twenty-two. Twenty-two cards in a single strike, each distributed by hand. It took him an hour to drive to the family. He handed out the cards like a man dealing blackjack, one up, one down,

—Bets, gentlemen. *Rien ne va plus.*

tipped his hat and left, leaving each Indian a magenta Jesus, left them staring at the halo and the azure sky, the white face and the yellow hair, wondering who the gringo was; and the man in the funny hat, waving and running now to his jeep, spinning wheels and careening off back to the main road.

News of Bicker's exploit was disclosed that night, when Deshais set about his ritual of opening the whisky bottle, summoning the ice, and settling himself in the large leather chair, feet up, wide smile, offering drinks all around. The talk was lively but Bicker hung back, a huge Scotch and soda in his fist, allowing the others to draw first blood. Brother Bicker waited for the second bottle to tell the others what he had done. He spoke very quietly in the beginning: "a triumph for counter-revolution," he called it; three hundred saved souls in a single day, twenty-two in a single round-trip bound. You should have seen their happy faces as they gazed upon the Saviour, Bicker said; watched their blessed mouths as they tried to *eat the cards*. Oh, it was a signal day for salvation, as great in its way as the devotion of Santa Theresa of Avila (he crossed himself). Next, he cried—Next, *I shall come down the mountain with tablets.*

Bicker, wound up, shaking his finger at Deshais across the whisky bottle, voice rising: All over the high plain this day there are saved souls, men, women, and children who have seen God, entered a state of grace, been prayed for, protected by the Holy Father, OBTAINED FAITH. It was Bicker's Fulton J. Sheen imitation, full of rolling rrr's and eyes cast upwards, Irish lilt, vestments gathered round him, damnation nearby, a solemn Latin invocation, *Sanctibus in omnibus suis* (he crossed himself again).

—No revolution can . . .

He paused, gathering breath.

— . . . MATCH THE REVOLUTION OF THE HOLY CARDS.

And the others waited.

—It is a thing all its own.

Bicker poured a fresh drink and was silent, his face red and wet from his labors and the emotion. The others stared into the high-ball glasses. There was a silence as the company puffed on cigarettes and rearranged their drinks, napkins. Deshais was grave for a moment, and then a small smile wrinkled his lips. Someone coughed, and then they all began to speak slowly and quietly, as if in a sickroom.

—Well.

—Yes.

—It's something.

—Ummmm.

—You . . .

— . . . had a strenuous day.

—Plain sometimes . . .

— . . . gets a man . . .

—down.

There was nothing else to say. The party tried to pick up where it had left off, but the conversation was lame and Bicker sat quietly drinking. Slowly the priests, brothers, and nuns gathered up their belongings and took leave. Reardon accompanied Bicker to his room, the elation all gone now; he left Bicker on the bed, staring wordlessly at the ceiling. Deshais said he would follow shortly.

Reardon returned to the apartment, wanting to tell the older priest to deal kindly with Bicker. But Deshais knew that. He was smiling and shaking his head; he had seen it before, in one form or another, and was sympathetic. It was common enough, really very common, and the end of the line for a missionary. The symptoms were familiar, but rarely did they occur so early in a man's service. With Bicker the evidence was everywhere, and they should have known. The height, Reardon; yes, the height.

"Problems, too," Reardon said.

"Height, Reardon."

"Indians," Reardon said, and meant that the problems of misery were so great that they could be solved only by one act of individual conscience to another, an act without regard for consequences or futures. There were no formulas at all, and no way to predict success. It varied with the man.

"Prayer," Deshais persisted. When a man deviated from prayer as the basis of his life, then the string was bound to unravel. It had to. There was nothing to count on except faith, Deshais said. It was Bicker's mistake to wander afield, and become too involved. But it had happened before and it would happen again.

Ten years ago in another part of the country (Deshais still told the scandalous story as a tragicomedy, with spiritual overtones; it was one of the stories that had worked its way into the lore of the mission, and was now just that: lore), Father Louis took to himself a wife, a crone from a mountain village who served him gruel and slept in his bed and joined in matins. Father Louis constructed a tiny altar of stone on the crest of a hill near their hut, and conducted services each day at dawn. He explained later to the doctors that if he could convert the crone, he could convert the entire high plain, could bring God into the lives of all the Indians. He dedicated himself to the woman and married her, as he had dedicated and married himself to God. The old woman represented all that he wanted, or would ever want. But she left him after a time, fled to join her son in the barrios, the slums of the capital. She left Father Louis without a word or gesture of explanation, and the old man awoke one morning to find the hut empty and no one for whom to conduct services. Despondent but determined still, he struck out across the plain that day (an hour's start on Deshais, who had at last located Father Louis and was in pursuit in the company of two husky Jesuits) and was found a week later, living with other Indians. He had achieved contentment of a sort, and was reluctant to leave. Deshais and the Jesuits found him round the cooking fire, adjusting the heavy chains which he now wore under his sackcloth. He told them that the problem, *the problem, padre, is that I cannot speak their language and they cannot speak mine, but we can signal, make signs to each other.* After a long, sad conversation they induced him to return to Acopara, and then under heavy escort he was taken to the capital. Father Louis was examined there by doctors, who recommended that he be taken to the United States for treatment. He was, and two years later died in Hartford. Deshais said a special mass in Acopara.

Bicker was on the same path, Deshais could see that. He was not a man suited to the climate. It was a question of balance. Deshais talked to Reardon for a moment, then went to Bicker's apartment. He found Bicker there, reading the Bible and smiling.

—Are you bothered by the height, Brother Bicker?

—I am bothered by the height, Father White.

Deshais ignored the name, ignored too the white tennis cap that Bicker had lately affected and now wore in bed. Deshais's eye took in the disorder. He arranged himself in a chair and proceeded.

—Tell me about the tablets. Which tablets are these?

—There are tablets.

—Yes.

—Well, they are there. Tablets. Of use.

—The tablets reveal the truth.

—Right.

—Ah, Brother Bicker. Do you believe you are useful here?

—No. Except for the distribution of holy cards, the most important thing I can do. Let me explain about the holy cards . . . they are here in the corner, in the whisky boxes, neatly stacked, as you can see. A grace. Can anyone say they are not a grace?

—Later, Brother Bicker. Now: What of the Indians? How can we help the Indians?

Deshais, avuncular, leaned forward, arms akimbo, hands on knees, staring at Bicker upright in the bed.

—*Print them in Acopara,* Padre. Print the holy cards in Acopara, where they belong. They will be cards native to the region.

—But . . .

—I believe the Indians are redeemed.

—Redeemed?

—Yes.

Deshais was deliberately formal, for a report would have to be made. It was tragic, really. But it would impress upon the authorities in Boston the true nature of conditions on the high plain, what could be expected and what could not.

—Brother Bicker, the Indians live by superstition.

—That is what I mean, Padre.

It was not a valuable dialogue. Deshais decided that Bicker must go. He was a man in the midst of a personal crisis, a faithful man in his own way, zealous—and that was just the trouble.

Bicker's delusions when they caught would spread like virus, unhinge the entire mission. He was dangerous, not serious in the manner in which a man must be serious to survive. So Bicker was recalled and Deshais, with Reardon, saddened. Bicker was the merriest of the lot, or had been up until the last weeks. He was a good and decent man, Deshais told Reardon; but not for here. Not for the plain. Not now.

They drove slowly through the crowded streets to the railroad station. The others knew nothing of the encounter with Deshais, only that it had not been successful and that Bicker was obliged to leave. Reardon parked the jeep in front of the station and was instantly surrounded by a dozen youngsters offering to take the bags. Bicker airily selected four of them, a pair for each bag, and the two of them walked to the platform.

They stood next to the train, both drinking beer, and Bicker said he really had enough of it, even after just six weeks, and was returning to the world, perhaps to the farm, perhaps someplace else. He felt he intruded upon the Indians; there was no place for him. Deshais and people like him were the only ones capable of running missions in a place like the plain; oh yes, he said, with a wave of his hand, you too, Reardon; you'll get along. But the others like himself, the others were malcontents, salesmen of lunacy. Bicker made Reardon promise he would continue to distribute the holy cards. Very important, Bicker said, between swallows. It does not matter that you are neither priest nor brother; I deputize you, Bicker said. It was the only important work that he did, very significant work, and he wanted to make certain it was continued. Reardon promised.

A minute to train time. The Indians with packs on their backs made for the coaches. Brother Bicker, his parlor-car ticket secure in his hatband, hung back, whistling to himself, finishing the beer. Finally he stuck out his hand.

"God bless."

"Luck," Reardon said.

"Keep Deshais on the straight and narrow." He had one foot on the platform and the other on the train steps. He was tipping his hat to the Indians that scurried past. "And keep cool, Reardon," he added.

"But what will you do now?"

"Distribute holy cards to the rich."

Reardon was walking beside the slowly moving train, and he looked at Bicker and laughed.

"Watch out for my Indians, Reardon."

"I'll care for them as if they were my own. Don't worry."

"Never mind the irrigation or the radio."

"Right."

"Or the model farm or getting them to mass."

"Right."

"Don't think about women."

Reardon nodded.

"I mean it: *Watch out for my Indians.*"

Reardon said: "God bless, Bicker."

He stood and watched the train move out of the station and around the curve, Bicker waving from the parlor car. The Indians who had collected on the platform began to disperse, the heavy bundles bending their backs, their faces blank. They made way for Reardon, carefully stepping out of his path as he walked slowly away from the platform and into the street.

It was ten o'clock and his mouth was sour from the beer. Bicker's decline had brought with it an appetite for alcohol, particularly beer before breakfast. He sat in the jeep, arms draped over the steering wheel. Life would become normal with Bicker's departure. The asylum had lost its most disturbing inmate. Now it would return to normal. He raced the engine, engaged the gears; time to get started, do what he used to do; time to get back to routine. He drove to the large stucco house where the nuns lived.

Reardon could hear the radio in the street, the morning news. He entered quietly, poured coffee, and greeted the sisters. They were all three of them pretty, looking like college girls with mussed hair and sleep in their eyes, and a careless way of talking that was acquired by people who lived close together. Sometimes when they were alone, the sisters called each other by their last names: *Jones,* hey, *Jones canya come here for a second?* There were no nuns' habits in Acopara, and never had been since the early days of the mission. It was tradition. So the three of them sat in print dresses and woolen sweaters at a long refectory table and ate corn flakes and boiled eggs and listened to the radio for news of the outside.

News: A collision of trains in Elizabeth, New Jersey, and a tax bill in the House of Representatives in Washington; the Holy Father journeying to Geneva on an ecumenical mission. They drank coffee and listened to the news, Sister Marie tapping a stainless steel spoon against the glass sugar bowl and grimacing at the details of the accident. Twelve killed, twenty-four injured; the railroad conducting an investigation; the governor, in a statement, shocked. The event was far-fetched, originating in Elizabeth, New Jersey, transmitted slow-spoken, monosyllabic, and assured by the Voice of America, short-wave. Each morning the sisters listened, and remembered, and verified what they heard with the worn copies of newspapers that came to Acopara. What was there to say of it?

"Tragic."

"What a terrible thing."

"Awful."

The sisters, like the morning news, were not permanent. They came in the winter of one year and left several seasons later, usually three years later. Thirty-six months on the high plain and then a return to the United States for a year and then off again: to the Sudan or Malaysia. They reckoned their time in the country by months, carefully ticking the calendars that hung in their rooms, the Pan Am Kodachromes of Maui or Venice or Rangoon. It was a volunteer tour of duty, but unlike the men of the mission, the priests and the lay brothers, the sisters seldom stayed on. At the end of two or three years, they left.

The newscast over, the women and Reardon turned to other things, details: where Reardon was driving that day, and how long he intended to be gone; the departure of Bicker. But Bicker had been turned over and examined, and re-examined, poked and prodded and dissected, a cadaver cut to pieces by expert pathologists. All there was left to say was that Bicker was gone, and all the sisters could reply was,

"Poor Bicker."

The sisters made the mornings pleasant for Reardon, who was uncomfortable at the mission, where he rented a room and took most of his meals. He knew and understood the spiritual, and preferred the secular. At the stucco house at the edge of town, the talk was slow and inconsequential, the sisters always cheerful and amused. Sometimes one of them accompanied Reardon on his rounds, explaining that it was beneficial to get out of town, to break the routine of church, orphanage, school, church, infirmary, school and church again. Partly, too, it was an excuse to lunch at a roadside café outside of town, and drink a beer and look at the mountains in the distance. Those were the best times, when it was almost possible to shrug off the mission and its projects, the Indians and the town, to talk of the taste of food or of family matters, to talk lightly and reminisce.

But the talk always came back to something involving the mission or the plain, or both, since the two were inseparable, two sides of the same face and more. Reardon liked the company of the sisters when he made his rounds, although there was little conversation on the road because of the noise the jeep made. But the sisters were always cheerful, almost too cheerful in a high-pitched way, shouting above the roar of the engine.

—The color of the mountains, Michael! Ooooo, look at the color of the mountains!
and alighting from the jeep before it stopped, to laugh with a child or speak in dreadful dialect with an old man. The sisters touched and charmed him with their conviction that sweetness of spirit perseveres; and he enjoyed driving with a woman. The sisters struggled to learn the dialect, and studied subjects like agronomy, to better understand the conditions of the plain. Some of them learned well, but it was obvious that no Indian (or any other inhabitant) took them seriously. It was as if they knew nothing at all, except how to pray and spread good cheer and be pleasant, to give breakfast to Reardon and comfort to the mestizo lady at the infirmary and instruction in English to the son of the dry-goods merchant. Accompanying Reardon on his rounds, the sisters found redemption in the tundra, and a justification for all their

lives. The tundra became beautiful in its desolation, and the life of the Indians noble in its adversity. The mission was there to do what it could, and the lives of the Americans therefore filled with grace; even Reardon, who had nothing directly to do with the mission, was neither priest nor brother, was included. He never challenged the sisters, because it was what they had and went by, but left it to Deshais, who enjoyed the correction of optimism, false hope he called it. Deshais warned the sisters to stay away from romantic conceptions of the Indians; life on the plain was nasty, brutish, and short, mostly nasty, and it was well they kept that in mind. And the sisters, fresh from a trip with Reardon, would smile. They did not think of themselves as romantics.

He finished the last of his coffee, and asked if anyone wanted to join him on his rounds. No one did. The sisters had other business. So Reardon left for his jeep and a normal day of business, a trip ten or fifteen miles up the road from Acopara; two or three regular calls, perhaps a call on a hut or two he had never visited. One waited to see what would turn up. On the twenty-ninth of every month, he filed a report to New York. The report began with progress on the irrigation project. He normally devoted a page and a half to that, his major investment of time and money; it was followed by commentary on developments at the radio station. The report ended in short paragraphs describing good works, a doctor found for this family, a small loan for that, a bit of machinery for the model farm. It was an informal report. Every six months he wrote a long summary, weighted with economic facts and figures, statistics largely of his own manufacture, plums on a bare tree. There were market prices and crop yields, and he had added a general price index and trotted that out every six months for the summary. It permitted him to make a comment beyond statistical data.

> The general price index remained stable, still in unfavorable balance for producers. But it is a buyer's market; the sellers have no place else to go and efforts this half, as the last half (see my 6/29), to improve the percentages have been unavailing... The cooperative, which began hopefully, is not functioning and I am redoubling efforts...

All the reports went to the shabby office in New York, where Smyth and Donnelly read them and made copies for their files. Reardon did not know what happened to the reports after that, although he was gratified once to learn that some of the facts and figures turned up in *The Congressional Record*. Reardon was admired for the brevity and objectivity of his style; no zealot, Smyth and Donnelly told the board. They had done tours in Latin America themselves, and knew the danger of zeal. The reports were concise and neat, well-typed, with no polemics or disputations; Reardon reported what he saw, and supported it with fact; sometimes he reported what he did. He did not betake himself on ideological excursions; he did not become involved, was not an advocate, and worked well with the mission, was well-liked by Deshais. The reports were useful, he was told, meaningful to the board of directors, each of whom received a mimeographed copy in the middle of every month. The document was marked: *Confidential*.

The Harris Foundation was not particular. It existed to siphon off excess profits from a cosmetics company, and its directors (a university president, a publisher, an architect, two lawyers, a former senator, a retired ambassador and three Harrises) did not inquire too closely into its activities. There were offices elsewhere in Latin America, four in all, staffed by Americans. Reardon was supplied with a budget of twenty-five thousand dollars, but ten thousand dollars of that went to him directly as salary, and some thousands more in expenses. He had the rest (as Smyth and Donnelly cunningly put it) to play with, although the total never seemed more than about five thousand dollars a year. The money dribbled away into insubstantial things, but the Foundation never complained. What the Foundation wanted at the end of each month was an accounting, and that was what Reardon gave them.

He thought about Harris as he left town, easing the jeep in low gear over the stones in the road, feeling the engine shudder and rush. If he told anyone he worked for Pretty Face Cosmetics Incorporated, they would not believe him. Why should they? Who would? But it was reasonable enough employment, decent, and permitted him to live outside the United States; when the time came to leave, he would leave. The next job would be no more difficult to find than this one, and this one had been easy. An introduction to Smyth from a friend, two expensive lunches in New York, and the information he was two years out of a monastery. He let that fall casually over coffee. Smyth and Donnelly looked quickly at each other, and after assuring themselves that there had been no scandal,

—No, ah, *problems* in the monastery?

—No. No problems.

—Real fine.

the bargain was sealed. Here was no fly-by-night, no eccentric or neurotic (though Reardon had held rather more jobs than was usual for a man of his age). Harris worked closely with the mission, on direct instructions from the senior Harris, who was a friend of Cardinals. Who better to work with Deshais than a man who knew the ropes, Smyth and Donnelly said. The last one didn't, and his tour ended in recriminations and a breach-of-contract lawsuit. Reardon was a man who could be depended upon, who would stick to his contract, last out the two-year tour, and if they were lucky sign up for another. And so Reardon was hired, and happily left America on the first available aircraft.

The jeep was out of town and climbing, its engine laboring in the ruts. Reardon carried a notebook in his pocket, and on the seat next to him a brown bag stuffed with holy cards. There were prayers in English, Spanish, and the Indian dialect, although few of the Indians could read. Fewer still were definitely Catholic, yet the children liked the pictures of Jesus (light-haired, white-skinned, sweet-tempered, Reardon thought; a prosperous Jesus). The adults understood that the cards were holy, and knew of no evil that could come from them. For the past month Reardon had given them out as he made his inquiries. The Indians accepted them as minor talismans, and put them away in safe places.

He drove five miles and stopped the jeep, leaving the engine running, and entered a hut by the side of the road. Reardon gave them plenty of warning he was coming, racing the engine, coughing loudly before knocking on the door. He entered at the invitation of the grandfather, who put out his hand in a vague gesture of welcome. Reardon had been there before, and recognized the family in the interior, the Indians smiling and nodding as he entered. He opened the bag and extracted the cards and passed them around—to the eldest first, ending with the youngest children and finally the infants. The grandfather did not collect all the cards right away, but he counted them so he would know how many there were; when Reardon left, he could collect them and put them away. The interior of the hut was small, dark, and rank with the smell of animals. The children were clustered around the fire, the mother off to one side, the father and grandfather standing stiffly near the door. *Lo peor es pedir:* the worst thing is to beg, so they stood tight, crouched bent and stiff because the roof of the hut was low and did not permit them to stand. Reardon squatted and took out his notebook and pen. He addressed the grandfather.

What is the price now of barley? In the market and in the countryside? Of potatoes? Of milk? What price will a grown llama fetch? The Indians regarded him with neutrality, and when he picked up one of the children and placed him on his knee, the child began to cry and the adults to laugh. Reardon smiled, and quickly put the child down again. What was your income last year? Last week? Last month? The old man scratched his head thoughtfully and consulted with his son. They were not sure. It would take them time to figure. Perhaps the padre could come back another time.

Over the pallet was a small crucifix, a gift from an earlier visit. The Indians followed Reardon's eye as he looked at it, nodded, and very swiftly crossed himself. The Indians followed suit. They thought he was a priest. And in mime:

—Are you well today?

—Fine, fine.

—No one is sick?

—Fine, fine.

—The little boy, sent to the infirmary?

—Okay. Ho-kay.

They did not know Spanish well enough to express what it was they wanted to say. So they said *bien, bien.* It might have been *mal,*

mal or any of a hundred other words. So much was withheld that Reardon took what he could, took what was visible and smiled back, offered the cards, tried to connect. He looked over the hut: it was genius: a man could not freeze, but neither could he be warm. It was a permanent underworld, neither this nor that, not murderous, not comforting, not a home but a shelter, and no more than a shelter. The Indians were cold today as usual and their hands, horny-skinned, moved to their faces and waited there, regarding Reardon. What would he do now? In the hut, Reardon's voice was low and quiet, equal to the remote and suspicious dignity of the Indians. The old man pointed to his wife and motioned for Reardon to approach and look at her.

She was an old and tiny woman, perhaps fifty, perhaps seventy; the years didn't matter. Her face was lined and dark as if carved from oak; an oaken figure, a fallen statue in the hut. She lay in the corner massaging her left foot, which was swollen and broken out in chilblains. The old woman was barely visible in the gloom. Reardon looked at her foot from a distance, then nodded gravely at the old man. The woman looked at him in fright and moved away, hoisting her body on her hands and scuttling further into the corner away from the door and the light and the stranger. It was painful: but the old woman had so many pains she could no longer distinguish among them, yesterday's from last week's or last month's. One pain blended into another, the pain in her stomach with the pain in her foot and the other pains. It was an infection. Reardon told the farmer, who did not need to be told what it was. It ought to be attended to by a doctor, who would examine and treat the old woman. Reardon said he would make the doctor come from Acopara; then he regretted saying anything. The Indians smiled when Reardon told them that the doctor would make the swelling go down with medicine. Or perhaps they did not understand what he was saying. It was impossible to tell.

—Fine, the farmer nodded. Fine.

—You will admit the doctor when he arrives?

—Yes, of course. But she will be well when the doctor comes.

Sure she will. Tomorrow or the next day a *paco* would arrive between noon and dusk, the best period for healing, and apply herbs and perhaps rub a dead animal over the woman's body, paying careful attention to the swelling on the foot. That would be if the disease required a *torca*, or exorcism of malevolent spirits. There were plenty of those in Acopara district, brought mainly by the wind which came from the south and west. In any case, whether malevolent or not, there would be herbs mixed with mutton fat and alcohol and rubbed on the body. That would come after the family had given the *paco* three large coca leaves, which would be read, and from the reading a diagnosis given. The treatment would cost about fifteen cents, or a few potatoes. There were nine varieties of potatoes in the district, and the *paco* could make his choice from any of the varieties grown by the farmer. Then he was given the coca to chew.

Reardon tousled the hair of one of the little children, who squealed and squirted out of the hut. The other children looked at him wide-eyed, the eyes enormous in the square brown faces. One of them moved behind Reardon and put a hand on his arm. Reardon did not feel the touch, but the child persisted. His arm was muscular, black with hair, and the Indians were smooth-skinned; they imparted forceful qualities to men with black hair on their arms. Reardon, nodding and smiling, backed out the door. Do not forget the old lady, he told the farmer. The grandfather was already collecting the holy cards, to put them away in a safe place. The child had his hand on Reardon's forearm, and he smiled and bent down and gave him another card.

—God bless, God bless.

—Fine, fine.

It had been done in under ten minutes.

That was Reardon's day. On other days he inspected the irrigation project or the radio transmitter or the model farm, all enterprises in which Harris had an interest, most of it marginal. He did not bring prosperity. In the beginning, he thought he could bring technology; know-how, as Smyth and Donnelly put it, to the high plain. He could bring a method, a manner of thinking to improve the grinding quality of life. Reardon figured that technology was the best of it,

—Look, irrigation. It means water all the time. You are not dependent on the sky!

—Fine, fine.

but then wasn't so certain. Even if he were able to convince the Indians of the superiority of his mind and his tools, his machinery and his logic, Reardon was not certain of the effect. To Bicker he had described himself as Pretty Face South, and of course went on with the job. Later he corrected his thoughts in his rational way to concern; solicitude for the Indians, nothing more. Later still, when time had passed and nothing had changed, when Reardon was enduring along with the Indians, he ceased to think about it in any specific way, content in the decently certain knowledge that he was not an agent of harm, was neither criminal nor cop; was not a subversive. So he loaded the jeep with holy cards. There was nothing that Reardon would do to change the lives of the Indians, and make him responsible therefore for their future or their fate. He did his job and enjoyed living at the mission. He walked through his rounds, beginning with coffee and the sisters, sometimes seeing visitors, then most days embarking with the cards to try to touch the Indians.

Driving the jeep to another cluster of huts, he thought that the holy cards were the constants in his life; he handed them out, gave them away, and relaxed. One, two, three: What are the prices of barley and milk; how's the family today; what's the income, last week? Last year? There were enough of Bicker's holy cards now to last for years, centuries perhaps. He visited two more families, then returned to Acopara in search of a doctor.

Reardon found Gutierrez in his rooms in the building adjoining city hall, drinking a cup of tea before resuming examinations of the patients that crowded his small anteroom. Reardon tried to talk to the doctor as if the conversation were not repeating itself for the tenth, the fiftieth time, all the old arguments shifting back and forth. Reardon sat in a chair in front of the desk while Gutierrez leaned back, casual and expansive. The trouble was that the Indians could not pay the doctors, except in goods, and it was not worth the trip for a few potatoes. Gas was expensive and time was even more expensive. The Indians: ah, the doctor told Reardon, they are always sick of one thing and another; they cure themselves; the *paco* cures them. You worry too much about the Indians, señor. Worry less about the Indians' health and more about their souls. They need prayer more than they need medicines.

Reardon explained about the old woman with the swollen foot, the chilblains, the infection, and the pain.

"How old is she?"

"Who can tell?" Reardon replied. "Fifty? Seventy? Who knows?"

"Leave it to the *paco*."

"It is not a long trip, Doctor Gutierrez. One hour, no more. I will drive you there myself, no need for you to use your own gasoline."

Gutierrez shrugged. "The old lady believes in the *paco,* not in me."

"And what do you believe in, señor?"

"Ah, prayer, not medicine. Salvation is the cure. You should tell your friends at the mission. It would do them good. They do not understand our ways. Get down to the soul of an Indian, and you will find a pagan. A savage!"

Gutierrez, a mestizo educated in the capital, a landowner, a politician, merchant, speculator, physician, giggled at his joke.

"It is the pagan in the Indian that must be cast out so that the soul can be saved. The souls are dead, and must be made to rise again. It is a job for the priests."

The doctor, convinced that spiritual health preceded physical health, was reluctant to visit Indians: the health of the Indians was a matter for physicians of the spirit. He drew an elaborate simile for Reardon's benefit. Then he laughed. Besides, being part Indian himself, the doctor was circumspect about the power of the *paco.* One never knew about *pacos.*

Nor of other things. Twice a week, after passing out holy cards in the morning, Reardon explored the plain alone, escaping the town, the mission, Deshais, the reports to Smyth and Donnelly. It was a pleasure to run the jeep off the road and take it as far as he could to the decayed and overgrown ruins to the east and the tiny pueblos that appeared miragelike on the horizon. The farther from Acopara, the wilder and less predictable the land and its people; the deeper into the interior, the greater the mystery. Cut off, surrounded by tundra and battered by wind, the land Reardon saw was lonely and unbelievably pure, of the character of the Russian steppes or the empty quarter of Arabia. He looked for Orthodox cathedrals but there were none; for Cossacks, but there were none of those either. There was a history, but where? The ruins were—ruins. There were no idols or sculpture, no inscriptions of any kind, no hint of what it was that had given life to the land and nourished a civilization. The ruins were only fallen buildings, lime-green moss covering the stones that toppled drunkenly to the ground, and overhead the big birds, riding wind currents, keeping ominous watch. Walking among them now: this was an aqueduct, that an assembly, the other—what?—a temple to the sun, an apartment? Possibly. Its symmetry haunted, the ruins at one with the land, constructed in perfect geometry. In the desolation, nothing was at war, all of it was one. Silence lay over the land with the air. He could drive for forty miles, seeing only a few herds of llamas or alpacas tended by youngsters. They looked at the car in puzzlement and fear, turning their heads away, ignoring him.

He brought a book with him one morning, intending to read it far out on the plain, spend all day with it, eat a lunch of sandwiches and beer, and return late, immersed in the land and the space and the words of the Russian. *In approaching the recent, very strange events that occurred in our hitherto rather unremarkable town, I feel that I must start further back by supplying some facts about the life of the gifted and well-respected Stepan Trofimovich Verkhovensky.* Reardon weighed the book in his hand, turned it over, thumbed its pages, glanced at the Afterword. Black and blue cover, close type. He hunched on the ground, his back resting against the jeep's tire, his knees tucked under his chin. The land he occupied was his own, the rest at bay. He tapped the book against his elbow like a castanet, and whistled a tune. One day, there would be a great American novel on a Russian scale about . . . technology. Know-how. America, the unterrible country, not susceptible to the Russian treatment, comprehensible only in bits and pieces, small boys or the self-exiled, small-town clerks who whored for the rich and became assassins. The great American technology novel would be written in numbers, and have the look of five-figure code. Six hundred pages of close type describing the rise and fall and rise again of a machine, a computer; a saga describing a family of computers, which ones succeeded and which did not, which married well and became successful corporation computers, and which languished in bowling alleys and at race tracks. It was a question of the programming, which was equipped to do what. There would be a patriarch, and a black sheep, a musician and an accountant. Yes.

But where were the American steppes? Ghettos perhaps, no doubt ghettos, unless you knew and understood the farmers south of Indianapolis, and had seen that country in December and January, in mid-winter. Anyway, they were not in Acopara or at the mission house or in the ruins tumbling down to the east; not in this space, unimaginably barren, where creatures coexisted with circumstance. Barren but sublime, marked by the wind and the rain but unmarked by man. The ruins were just another random pile of stones, moss-carpeted, open.

In approaching the recent, very strange events. He tried to read. Reardon pushed up against the tire and opened the book, but the words refused to focus. The sentences nudged each other, and his mind was torn from concentration, his eyes focused outward, not to the sky but to the land. So empty was it that he closed the book after a few lines, nervous and apprehensive that he was being watched, watched as the sun is reflected in a water drop, although there was no house or tree or animal in sight, only the wind and the space and the high clouds in the sky; and the book opened in front of him. The horizon came up to meet him, and he put the book down, closed it, and began walking. Reardon commenced to talk aloud, and then he was wandering in front of the jeep.

He waited for the echo. The wind came from the horizon and he felt it on his face, the wind mixed with dust. His eyes were black with distance, the mountains in his eyes measured in a hundredth of an inch. Teetering, balance awhack, gone, no sense of up or down, Reardon stumbled like a drunk in a drawing room, afraid of the breakage. He looked about now, and tried to assemble what he had: there was the book. He nudged a small stone with his shoe, scraped it from the earth and kicked it, followed and kicked it again, picked it up and looked at it, and threw it hard at the horizon, watching it hit at the end of the world, bounce twice, and come to rest. He scrambled back to the jeep and read aloud, from memory, in a whisper: *I feel I must start further back by supplying some facts about the life of the gifted and well-respected Stepan Trofimovitch Verkhovensky.* The words lived briefly, then died, and he stood motionless, listening for an echo or a reply.

There was nothing to hear. He was alone, no menace. The jeep was there, ready. Reardon, jaunty now, shook his head and began to laugh. He kicked at a stone, put his face to the sky. Then he walked slowly back to the jeep and picked up his things, the pack and the lunchbox, and leaned on the windshield. He pitched the things into the back seat, climbed in, raced the engine, and moved off, scattering dirt under the wheels. The terror vanished, erased by the roar of the engine. Reardon was secure when moving, drifting in the car to no certain destination. He never took the book to the plain again, nor did he stop alone. Driving without plan, he found settlements where no priest had ever been, nor government agent either.

There was a town thirty miles from Acopara, approached as a

treeless oasis of mud huts, paths cut among them haphazardly, as if by afterthought. It was a town without relieving ornament of any kind, no color and no oddity, a town as gray and menacing as a rotting carcass. Most of the houses were empty of furniture or personal things, yet in daytime there were people; and stray cats. In the beginning, Reardon was drawn to it—God knows why; because it was inexplicable; perhaps because of its mystery. People collected in doorways or in the town's only café and watched the jeep. It was a town of no commerce, living a life of its own unconnected with anything except the land it occupied. The people of Acopara stayed away. They would not explain why. They would only say it was a bad place. The mayor of Acopara, a mestizo, told Reardon it was a pueblo filled with bandits. But Reardon replied he had never had any trouble of that kind, and had never heard of anyone who had. All right, the mayor shrugged; it was still a place to stay away from. Perhaps not bandits, he said then; "Indians of a different sort," and gave no further explanation. At night, did the people slip away into the mountains to reappear at early morning? There were no children underfoot, or in the houses, or in the footpaths that ran beside the houses; nor were there animals, except for the cats.

Reardon avoided the town from the day he followed a funeral procession. The horses, hung with black cloth, erupted from an alleyway without warning and Reardon, driving slowly and carefully between the houses, halted. A line of horses came from the alley in slow sullen file, mounted by men dressed darkly; no one looked at the jeep or at Reardon. In the center of the procession was a small horse cart and on the cart a body tightly wrapped in red cloth, laid lengthwise, small and unobtrusive. The windows of the houses were empty, and the streets, too; there was nothing

save the procession, moving in small steps which became a cadence on the rough road. Reardon turned off the engine of the
jeep, and climbed out and followed on foot. The cart with its burden lurched from side to side as its wheels caught in the ruts. A
team of horses led the cart, itself shrouded in black, the cloth hitting the dirt as the wheels lurched and turned slowly. All of this
was in silence, except for the sounds of the wood and the wind
that flapped the cloth and brought up dust from the path. The
wind rose as the procession moved out of town, past the huts and
up the path that forked to the mountains. The men on horseback
adjusted their ponchos, wrapping them around their faces to ward
off the wind and the cold. Their bodies bent against the wind slipping and moaning down the slopes of the hill. There was no priest
or *paco;* no leader or a family to mourn the dead. There was a
corpse and a cart and the men of the town to escort it to burial,
and Reardon on foot walking behind. In the darkness of an over-
cast day there was malevolence in the procession, the summoning
of a curse in the long file of men and horses; death was in the
houses and in the twisted shrubs along the path, in trees along
with the buzzards; and in the wind. Perhaps it was something that
happened a millennium before, so deep had melancholy spread itself in the town. Reardon watched it carefully, a stranger. He followed for an hour, until the horses reached the fork. They halted
there and the riders turned round to face him. They remained
until he retreated a few steps, then backed off toward the town.
Then they resumed march, walking slowly off into the mountains, Reardon watching them, the horses lurching and the men
sitting easily in the saddles, their fingers holding the reins loose,
bending with the wind that came down the slope. Reardon
walked slowly through the town back to his car, looking into the

windows and the alleyways between the houses. He saw an old woman standing in the alley where the horses had come from, watching him. She put out her hand, and Reardon gave her a few pennies. Who are the people who live here? Where do they come from? The old lady shook her head; she did not understand. Who is being buried? He pointed up the mountain.

"Dead," the old woman said.

"Who?"

"Dead," she shrugged, *"muerte,"* looking at him coldly and walking off up the alley, tucking the coins in her pocket. Two cats followed, and she turned every few feet to look at them and at Reardon.

"What is the name of the town?" Reardon called after her, a useless question. What did it matter?

She shook her head and kept moving, and finally disappeared at the end of the alley. The town was empty again, and Reardon wrapped his poncho tightly around his shoulders. Somewhere a shutter banged as it turned on a hinge. The silence was oppressive as Reardon climbed into the jeep. He drove it to the fork in the road and looked to the hills, trying to find the procession. He thought he made it out, then decided that what he saw was dust; that, or a shadow in the hills. He sat looking into the distance for a long time, the noise of the engine drowning out the wind. The file of men had got lost among the rocks, and there was no sign of it now.

Chapter Two

DESHAIS WAS SAYING MASS in the small chapel and could not be heard at the entrance to the church. When Reardon approached the main altar, he heard the weak voices of the congregation, a murmur that slid toward him and washed over the altar and the benches. Noon, and there were a dozen mestizos kneeling on the stones, resting their heads on the backs of the wooden pews. Reardon crossed himself and stood and watched the service, his hands on his hips. The midday rain drummed at the windows, its cold smell inside the church, on the clothes of the mestizos, clinging to the stones, the altar and the priest. The main window was dark, the stained-glass with its round Rivera-like figures of Indians and animals muted and run together, smeared by the dark light. Mestizos came in the morning in coats and ties, and this was a service attended by some who had come late to market.

Deshais performed it: Deshais with his quick, precise movements, his Pope Pius head on Dylan Thomas body, his vestments like plumage in the gloom of the chapel. Deshais was reading from Matthew.

> *How blest are those who know they are poor;*
> *The Kingdom of God is theirs.*
> *How blest are the sorrowful;*
> *They shall find consolation.*
> *How blest are those of a gentle spirit;*
> *They shall have the earth for their possession.*

Deshais spoke the words very clearly and precisely from the altar, looking at the people on the benches. They were old, elderly men and women who came in black with lined and solemn faces; perhaps they came in to get in from the cold. In the rear, the back row, were two Indians, both women, who sat stolidly and listened to the words, moving their lips, concentrating. The young men were elsewhere, out in the fields or in the mountains beyond the fields. They had heard Matthew before, too often. But it affected Reardon: the lone man splendidly arrayed before the simple altar, the congregation before him, mumbling a hymn that was only partly understood. Deshais was the church in all its history and in the majesty of raiment and buildings, confident, ancient—there now, in the small chapel, a dozen worshippers, Deshais, the altar, the church. It all came down to that.

Reardon stood and watched the service. Was Deshais ministering to the dead? The Sermon on the Mount: the words blended with the sound of the rain, words for a rainy day. Sentimental words. Reardon believed them for a lot of complicated reasons, but mostly because he could afford to believe them; he believed them in the distance. They were decent and generous words, but he could not understand how the poor, the sorrowful, or the meek believed them. It was more than fear. Why would an Indian woman accept the Sermon on the Mount? But then, why did anybody accept anything? Whose sermon? Whose mount? The image didn't fit. The Jesuits understood it, understood too that the King James Version was a little more ambiguous and a little less ironic.

> Blessed are the poor in spirit:
> For theirs is the kingdom of Heaven. . . .
> Blessed are the pure in heart:
> For they shall see God.

A little milder, that one. Not quite so disturbing, its edges were shaved, blunted; a more beautiful poem, but a less radical sentiment. The other was a sermon for Jesuits and revolutionaries; it was really a revolutionary code, surprising that the government permitted it to be read, didn't require King James in the churches. If Deshais were Ché, it would sound completely convincing; what Deshais needed was a new suit of clothes, a beard perhaps, and a rifle; a black beret and a clenched fist. But the Indians: how could the Indians listen to it, either version really, when everything they saw and heard and felt refuted it? It was a denial of reality. Well, there were no Indians in the chapel, except the two ladies in black, mourning, in perpetual mourning, stroking crucifixes and listening.

> The Lord be with you.
> And with thy spirit.
> Let us pray.

The congregation descended to its knees with a rustle, and Reardon crossed himself again. Well, he thought, we would know about it in two years or three, know for certain when something came to replace the church and cancel Matthew—cancel him or revive him, depending on who or what the something was. When the priests were replaced by others and driven out. It would take them two years to move, to infiltrate the necessary equipment and more than equipment, confidence. They needed a leader, just one, and not Father Francis or any of Father Francis's people; one man, someone like Zapata, someone who could hate and who understood the conditions. Then perhaps the revolution could be successful in its own terms. It had not worked spectacularly well elsewhere, but nothing else had either. Of course that wasn't the question; the revolution was coming, was there, and was there regardless. Reardon looked at the people on their knees and Deshais at the altar. It was something, but at what cost? What is the price for that? The price was high everywhere, a matter of which rot you preferred, ours or theirs; men were what mattered, not equipment and not even theory. Or theory least of all. When there were enough guns and men prepared to use them, where would God and His priests stand? How soon would they be replaced? Or would they be permitted to remain as museums of natural history, living fragments found among the rubble.

—*Look, Chico. This is a priest. See his clothes. See the cross he has in his hand. Look at the book. It is a Bible. Look at the priest with the cross and the Bible.*

If God and his priests did not work, the guns would. The question answered itself. One bondage was the same as the other, with a moral at the end of it. The church on the plain was at the edges of human existence, neither essential nor connected to the reality, although it endured by its authority and its revelation of the past and what it was able to promise in the future. One would watch to see whether the new answers served better than the old; or not new answers, other answers. But there were no guns or leaders or a revolution in the chapel, merely old people in out of the rain and the cold, looking at the altar, following Deshais.

Reardon watched silently from the side, worrying it. After the priests came the other foreigners, the advisers, *consejeros;* the ones on loan, the new missionaries. They were there now, from North America and Europe, men on loan from other continents; on loan; lent. Rented for an afternoon or a year or twenty years. Expertise. Build a power plant or a highway, or find the coal in order to build a mine. Yes, expertise.

—*Look, Chico; this is a technical adviser. Look at his slide rule. See the papers he carries in his hand. It is a plan. The technical adviser has a slide rule and a plan.*

And money, always money. Of course money, by grant or loan or bushel basket. Plans without money were just . . . plans. The advisers would be stuffed and mounted and stuck into the museums in a wing of their own, down the hall from the priests; they would have a diorama of their own, and a tinselly history of their monuments. The General Price Index was Exhibit A, next to a perfectly preserved transistor radio.

Reardon felt the wet in the church, and stood listening to Deshais. They were bowed now, praying. For the moment it was futures. No one knew anything for certain, least of all the men at the mission. But there were rumors. It was a wonderful country for rumors. A few men were said to come across the border to the west, bringing guns with them. There was talk that a guerrilla had already been formed, and was camped high in the hills. The trouble was that talk never came from the people, it came from foreigners like Reardon and Bicker who wanted it to happen, and after a time were unsure whether they overheard the rumors that they spread, or thought them up themselves. There were reports in American magazines and newspapers, God knows where they came from. What could a newspaperman know that someone living in the middle of it could not? None of it was verified. At least, Reardon could learn no details, and he had made attempts to learn.

A month after Reardon arrived in Acopara, Deshais asked him to lunch with the American military attaché, a blunt lieutenant colonel of infantry in for the day from the embassy in the capital. The visitor was reserved at lunch, choosing his few words with care, and refusing drinks. Deshais did most of the talking, spinning anecdotes about the Indians, complaining about the weather, and inquiring into conditions at the embassy. The lieutenant colonel was noncommital; he wanted to know about the army garrison outside of town, and particularly about the major who commanded it. But Deshais did not know him, nor did Reardon. At the end of the meal, the lieutenant colonel asked Reardon if he would accompany him to the garrison; an interview with the major had been arranged, and he needed someone to translate.

It was an elaborate meeting. The lieutenant colonel and Reardon were greeted with fanfare, a color guard and the major standing on the steps of the compound, as if it were the president of the republic or the chief of the joint staff. Inside, the major offered drinks, Coca-Cola and beer, introduced his aide, and initiated a half hour of chatter through which the lieutenant colonel sat bored and impatient, twisting the West Point ring he wore on his third finger, left hand. The interview began with a question from the American. He wanted to know the major's estimate of the guerrilla threat to the plain, specifically to Acopara.

Reardon translated.

The major said there were Communists in the hills, not enough to cause serious trouble yet, but growing and supplied by rebel elements across the border; a rebellion externally supplied and supported and (naturally) encouraged. It was growing, and if steps were not taken, there would be trouble in the near future; it must be dealt with now, and dealt with decisively, since movements like this one never stayed small. Conditions encouraged growth. There were too many grievances, real or imagined, the colonel said; and these, despite the best efforts (a nod at Reardon) of American aid. The major alluded vaguely to skirmishes, and said that one rebel had been wounded in a battle and was taken prisoner, but (*¡Qué lástima!*) that he died while in transit to the garrison for questioning. The military attaché listened closely as Reardon translated, transcribing all of it on a pocket tape recorder and making notes as well.

—So how many are there?

—It is difficult to tell, colonel. One band, perhaps two, of some size, we think. At least of platoon strength, perhaps larger. Perhaps as large as a company.

—And who is their leader?

—We are not certain. A document . . .

—Yes?

—. . . one document we have indicates he may be Cuban. But then again, perhaps not.

—And the others?

—They are peasants, rabble.

—Local people?

—Local or not local, rabble.

The major spoke very slowly and cautiously, for he had been carefully rehearsed at joint staff headquarters in the capital. It was a delicate interview. The threat must be presented as grave, but not too grave; minor now, but potentially serious. One must take care not to feed rumors. The major, worried, spoke alternately to the whirring tape recorder, to the military attaché, and to Reardon. He had not been told Reardon was coming, and now he thought that probably Reardon was working for the embassy. Then he slid back the desk drawer, and brought out a piece of paper. He smoothed the wrinkles from it, and passed it across to the attaché.

—You see, there is a reference to the twenty-sixth of July movement, and there again a reference to Eutimio Guerra. This is a document we found on the prisoner.

The lieutenant colonel turned it over in his hands. It was a piece of cheap notepaper, ragged at the edges, as if torn from a pad.

—What is a eutimio guerra? Some kind of war?

—What? No, Colonel. It is not a war, it is a person. Guerra was a guide for Castro in the early days of the Sierra Maestra. He was loyal to the government and nearly succeeded in delivering the Castro gang into the hands of the authorities. It might have been ended then, but he was betrayed and the Communists killed him. You see here, the prisoner makes reference to Eutimio Guerras; he means traitors.

The lieutenant colonel nodded, made notes, and passed the paper back to the major.

—Do you have an estimate of their equipment, their armament?

—The prisoner we captured had a Thompson.

—A Thompson?

—I can show it to you, Colonel. The prisoner said before he died that his group was to receive . . . weapons from, ah, Communist Europe. He spoke of Czech weapons.

The major shifted uneasily, and smiled, pushing a pack of American cigarettes across the top of the desk. The lieutenant colonel refused them with a wave and, writing swiftly, grunted that he would like to see the Thompson. It was produced presently, and the two of them discussed it for a few moments, hefting it and sighting it, looking for markings. The colonel noted the serial number. They stood before the desk debating its value vis-à-vis the M–16. They joked lightly, and the interview ended.

Impressed with the major's manner as well as with his arguments, the attaché on his return to the capital arranged for a small shipment of arms to the garrison at Acopara. It was an informal transfer, a down payment, a hundred or so .30 caliber machine guns, a few grenade rifles, and half a dozen mortars and ammunition for them. He sent along a new sidearm for the major as a personal gift. More arms would follow, if the embassy could get the necessary authorization; meantime, the lieutenant colonel wanted every scrap of intelligence the major could give him. The weapons sent were not new or modern, but they were serviceable and were better weapons than the models the major had. The attaché and Reardon had been given a full tour of the garrison's armory, and the absence of heavy weapons was carefully noted. The position, as the major pointed out, was difficult in the event of a sustained attack, particularly an attack where the enemy had artillery of any kind; his own automatics and mortars were old, and there were not enough of them. Ammunition was rationed, and the men were not properly drilled. It was all very difficult. The garrison was vulnerable.

In Acopara, there were rumors of arms shipments, but Reardon did not learn definitely of them until much later. Deshais, deep in his cups at the mission one night, told him the story. They

had sat up late arguing, trying to get straight the relationship between the army and the people. The government brought in the
army and told it to sit on the edge of town in a garrison. The soldiers were not permitted leave, so their contact with the people
was slight. They occupied a garrison, an outpost, and guarded—
what? An invasion. An attack. Who knew? They sat there, six hundred men and a major, the government presence in Acopara and
the plain. When someone important visited, they mounted a
color guard. Every month they were paid. With reluctance, Deshais told Reardon the story of the guns.

"*Mira*," Deshais said, using the single Spanish word he understood absolutely; it laced his sentences together. "Look: the government wants guns. It has wanted them for twenty years. What
they've got now is cast-off junk. We haven't given them any, God
knows why. Probably an oversight. But that meeting of yours and
the colonel's did it. For the first time, there were details."

"What details?"

"A Cuban-born leader, Michael. Cuban-born. A Thompson submachine gun. An armed rebel band. A prisoner and a document, a
real piece of paper with writing on it *in Spanish*. Eutimio Guerra.
It might as well have been Lenin. C'mon, Michael. You see that."

"Yeah," Reardon said. "Sure."

"Okay. It was more than just someone saying it. It was facts, details. First you had a theory, and now you've got facts. Listen: after
they fed that lieutenant colonel the details, they passed on their
own evaluation that all of it, this revolution, was in the incipient,
potential stage, the stage where it could be nipped in the bud, the
baby . . ."

". . . strangled at birth," Reardon said. The phrase was familiar.

"Right. All they needed was the guns. No troops, no manpower, just guns. One of the sons of bitches even quoted Churchill. 'Give us the tools and we will finish the job.'"

"Christ," Reardon said.

"The threat. Now they had a real, live threat." Deshais barely contained his laughter. He was up now on the edge of the leather chair, drink in hand, pointing his finger at Reardon's nose. "They said the threat was external, like the border was the Yalu. The Americans ate it up. *Ate it up.* They gave them a few airplanes, too, but that's another story. One of them even flew up from the capital to ask me what I thought."

"Well?"

"Nah, I told them. The Indians're half dead. It would take a lot more than a couple of Cuban machine guns to stir them up."

"Czech," Reardon said.

"Check who?" said Deshais.

"Not Cuban, Padre. Guns from Czechoslovakia. God knows why they chose Czechoslovakia. That's what the major told the attaché."

"Well, anyway, I was negative."

"But they didn't believe you."

"What the hell, Michael. They are not paid to believe me. So they didn't. But it was one reason Gaskell came."

"One plague deserves another," Reardon said.

"Well, someone had to do the independent evaluation."

Reardon sat looking at Deshais, not saying anything.

". . . and it was from Gaskell that I know what happened, so lay off Gaskell."

"Shit," Reardon said.

"It was the details," Deshais went on, back in his chair now, legs stretched under the coffee table. His fingers were steepled under his chin. "The details had to be verified. It's funny when you think about it. You had to have a verified Cuban with a verified Thompson."

"But who gave the verification?"

"Gaskell, for God's sakes. It was Gaskell, and a clever job it was, Michael. You have to admire the technique. You have to admire it."

You sure did. It was something to be admired, all right. Reardon was not certain of that. What he knew was that Gaskell had come and made a difference, perhaps the crucial difference in the decision to arm the garrison. Not that even that made any real difference. A non-guerrilla was no better or worse facing modern weapons than ancient ones. The guerrilla was no closer to existence either way. But the guns were the first premonition of an active American interest in the plain; the flag usually followed the guns. Gaskell preceded the guns, which preceded the flag.

Gaskell arrived from the River Institute on contract to the Department of Defense, a lean economist, dressed in olive-drab trousers and an army field jacket. Gaskell had been advised to stay away from the mission, but in time he was drawn to Deshais. He and Deshais became friends, and late at night over drinks, while Gaskell made notes, Deshais told him of the guerrilla Communists in the hills near Acopara. That is, there were none that Deshais knew of; but the priest was careful to add, *mira,* that he did not get around as much as he used to. But those natives with whom he spoke agreed with him. Gaskell was disconcerted by Deshais's observation, and pressed him on it.

—Who could live in a place like this without being a Communist?

—Strange but true.

—I don't believe it. You've been here too long, Padre. It takes a man with fresh eyes to spot the threats.

—Threats?

—That is what worries them in Washington. The threats. In countries like this one, the threats are everywhere. It makes Washington nervous.

—You're kidding me.

— . . . the trick is to spot them. No people could live in conditions like these without contemplating revolt. Q.E.D., Padre. Root out the threats, is the job we have.

—You bet. But odd as it sounds, there are no Communists here. But ask someone else. Ask Reardon.

—It isn't plausible.

—Ask Reardon.

—What Reardon doesn't know about the dynamics of revolution would fill an encyclopedia.

—Well, it's the truth anyway.

—We'll see.

Gaskell was scrupulous in his interviews, making lengthy notes and always taking care to judge the political attitudes of his respondents. In the evenings, he retired to his room at the mission to type up the findings, which went into black notebooks and were locked in a filing cabinet when Gaskell was absent. They were described as "the goods," and grouped under headings; Reardon's interview was in the DOUBTER file. Evidence, as Gaskell soon discovered, was nonexistent. But the intuition was overwhelming. Gaskell was a man who had come to distrust facts, and so relied almost wholly on instinct. He looked at terrain like an oil prospector, seeking to discover what lay below the surface. Hunch governed—that, as Reardon sourly observed, and the requirements of the contract. Gaskell proceeded to write his initial report, a paper which had as its epigraph a quotation from Deshais to the effect that life on the high plain was nasty, brutish, and short.

His judgment was that an insurgency of major implications could be expected in the near future. Men were gathering in the mountains and they were externally supplied and supported. What was contemplated was a classic war of national liberation along the lines of those others so depressingly familiar in recent history. The vehicle was a guerrilla band whose security was so tight, its organization so disciplined, that the name of the leader was not yet known. But it was armed with Thompson submachine guns, and a shipment of Czech weapons was reported en route. Economic and political conditions on the plain were bad and getting worse, deteriorating, and since there was very little chance of improving the conditions, efforts must be made to eliminate the rebels. There might be variations on that, Gaskell wrote, but the main fact was this: the time was late, the priority urgent, the threat definite. Independent analysis confirmed it. Gaskell ended his list of tentative recommendations with the thought that the Institute be given funds to undertake a major study, with a full-time fieldworker and two researchers. Office space was available.

The report alarmed the embassy, but as the ambassador noted in a critique, the logic was inescapable; it hung together. The military attaché agreed with all of it. Gaskell himself was treated with unusual courtesy at the embassy, when he came to call after the long weeks in Acopara. Over drinks at the residence, the ambassador assured him that the Institute would be asked to maintain a presence on the high plain. A contract was assured.

"We've got the goods," Gaskell said.

"Wonderful. When do you set up shop?"

"Soon, pretty soon. But I think it had better be here, not in Acopara."

"Oh. Why?"

"Well, you know."

"No, seriously. Why?"

"Communications," Gaskell said with a wink.

And the attaché sent the guns.

Reardon stood by the altar and watched the service, thinking about Gaskell, now long gone, and about the Indians, the rumors. He looked again for the Indian women in the rear pew, but they were gone; they had left before the end of the service. Then, as the congregation began its prayers, Reardon left the main altar and went on through the church to the alley behind it, and climbed the outside stairs to Deshais's apartment, where the others were.

The others. Four priests, three nuns, three laybrothers, all in street clothes. No one wore the dog collar now, except at mass and occasionally when important visitors called. In Deshais's apartment, they stood with their backs against the bookcase or sat in the plywood chairs drinking Coca-Cola and beer, quiet and waiting. It was as if the height had drained their vitality, left them pale and uncertain. The two guests there for lunch sat and listened politely, and the silence between words was audible and measured in inches.

"Cold. It's cold in September."

"Good to be inside." Smile.

". . . in September."

"The place needs . . ."

Sigh. ". . . more heat."

"Electric heaters. They're selling electric heaters now."

"Too expensive."

"Ummmm."

"Better." Pause. "Better than the cold."

"Sure."

". . . dry cold."

"High, dry cold."

Father Francis offered cigarettes to the visitors.

"The singing's stopped."

"Colder this year than last."

"Oh, I don't think so."

"That never changes."

"The cold is the same."

". . . never changes."

"The rooms are all right, with the . . . heaters."

"When you can find them."

"The heaters do a good job."

"The electric ones."

"When you can find them."

"Has someone a light?"

"It's worse on the plain."

Some had been in Acopara for fifteen years and more, and they reminded you of soldiers in a war. It was a way of life, neither better nor worse than other lives, but the one that there was. It was not easily explained to outsiders, the details open to endless refinement, reflections in a long row of mirrors. There was a private mythology, limits too, as in an army, and these were a security. It was the life they lived with and talked about, bounded on one edge by the church and on another by the town and on a third by the plain. There was a road and a railroad station, and the people. And now books, the new ones sent from Boston and brought by the young men who replaced the old. *The Stages of*

Economic Development. Take-off Point. Technological Change. Technol-ogy and Culture. Tradition.

If religion did not seem . . . appropriate, take a shift to econom-ics. A full stomach preceded a state of grace. For St. Paul, substi-tute Gunnar Myrdal. It was another catechism, the substitute for the rose window or the new altar, and the closest thing to revolu-tion the church had known. The direction of zeal moved to higher ground, all of it new, barely broken, surrounded by uncertainty. Split the life into two parts, one part for the fallen and the other part for the institution. The institution informed and bounded it, kept the fence closed. Hang on to your own faith, and do what you can for those with no faith. The routine began and ended with prayers, and in between times you did what you were sent out to do: help. Priests' black awed the natives, so you did away with it.

—See, we are just like you now.

—Fine, fine.

Stay well away from dogma, it was not pertinent. It did not meet the needs of . . . of the priest or of the flock. "Discover the places where the spirit is already at work," was the way Brother Irwin said it, and did not go farther. He sought the spirit. The men of the mission worked at it without enriching themselves in any ma-terial way and ended up better for doing it. The job was personal, lonesome, and what worked for one man failed for another. But sooner or later the conscience tilted and shifted, and finally set on a knife's edge. Then it was a matter of motive.

—Padre, what do I do? *What do I do now?*

—It may be God's will.

—Perhaps, certainly. But what *do I do?*

—We will make inquiries . . .

—My boy has gone to the capital, and you won't find him. No one will. Who will support me now?

—You have relatives.

—None here.

—Well, go to them anyway.

—Perhaps you could give me a little money, Padre.

Reardon had stood to one side, listening. The padre, Peter Francis, stood in front of the woman clasping and unclasping his hands. She was looking at him directly.

—We have very little money here.

—I do not need much, a little.

—A very little.

—To get by.

—Yes.

—Until the boy comes back. Until my family . . .

—I understand, but . . .

—. . . can help.

—Yes. God's will.

—I will come to mass every day, then.

—Every day?

—For a very little money, to live.

—Trust in God.

—Yes, Padre.

In Deshais's apartment late at night they worried and talked about Reardon, who moved through the landscape with no plan and no motive, moved only to keep going, to keep it all at arm's length. He drafted reports and sent them elsewhere. All the methods had been tried, he told them one night, and none seemed to work. So he settled himself into a comfortable scheme, a way of moving through the china shop without breaking anything. He told them it reminded him of half a year he spent abroad, up each morning at nine, to the café for coffee and brandy at ten, reading to one, lunch to three, nap until five, read until seven, dine until ten, talk until two, sleep to nine, when the day began over again. He managed to finish his reading of the nineteenth-century Russians just that way—and what have you done lately to equal the reading of Pushkin? Coffee and cognac, coffee and cognac, a little talk, some food, some rest, some reading, and a quiet sleep. See, Reardon had said; see, it works. *Mira.*

The rest of them, obliged to connect, thought Reardon a strange sort. Why here? Why now? They were not enlightened. Reardon was available, did not complain, was not offensively cynical. He helped. Deshais, at night, pouring a drink, would turn to Reardon and purr: Tell us about the monastery, Michael. How many years there, five years? Six? In Ohio, wasn't it? Deshais waited, with the others. All the stories were forced out, in one form or another. Then the talk passed on, but Deshais waited quietly, because he knew it would come round again.

So they came and went, the missionaries, long-distance commuters, Bicker and his holy cards, the laybrothers fresh from business careers, thence to the plain and afterwards to Africa or an Indian reservation in America. Connoisseurs of misery, Bicker had said in a light and unkind moment. And at the center of it was Deshais, holding it together, enduring to prove that he could, hanging on and prevailing.. And all of them linked to Reardon, the one from the outside, the one who nodded yes, of course; let's get the job done. The job. Whatever it is.

The conversation was so low, so quiet, it was inaudible on the stairs. Reardon felt like tiptoeing into the room, turning himself invisible by effort. The guests for lunch were an American engineer, on loan for a week to assist in a government project outside of town, and a government official who worked in city hall. The engineer was stiff and formal, correct in the presence of the clergy; the government official, Cortes, was plainly bored. Reardon was introduced to the engineer, and shook hands with Cortes. Then he excused himself and went into Deshais's kitchen, where the beer was.

Francis followed him, and they joked for a minute about Deshais's full larder. The refrigerator was stuffed with beer and canned goods, prepackaged soups and stews and diet preparations. Below, in the vegetable tray, were three bottles of Russian vodka. Reardon took one of them and hefted it, and the bottle misted over and became very cold to the touch. In the large room, the talk went on, low and quiet.

". . . is there much missionary work done here?" It was the engineer. He added, "to proselytize . . . "

Reardon muttered to Father Francis that the question required an answer from Brother Bicker. Only Bicker could give it the attention it deserved. Francis frowned. Bicker was not his favorite laybrother, past or present, not in the beginning and not even at the collapse at the end. He had sympathy but not respect. A basic lack of sense, of seriousness about the high plain had been Bicker's trouble. Francis pulled the pop-top on a can of Budweiser and handed it to Reardon.

"You must see how poor the people are, how terrible the disease is," one of the sisters said. She spoke quickly and lightly, in a high and passionate voice. "There are services, Communions, and the work of the church goes on. But..." She shrugged, and turned to Cortes, the government man, slouched against the bookcase reading a magazine.

"Many of the Indians are Catholic," Cortes said, speaking English with a heavy accent. "The Spanish influence is still large, perhaps the largest of all." He spoke into the pages of the magazine, not looking up.

"An influence," Father Francis said from the door, a can of beer in his hand.

"To understand the country, study the Spanish," Cortes said.

"It will tell you a lot about economics," Francis said.

"The people," Cortes said slowly.

Francis, in a low voice, answered: "What the señor means is that many of the Indians do not accept the church if we bring it to them." He paused, and added: "They do not refuse us necessarily."

"What do you mean?" asked the engineer.

"The problem here is with the . . . outsiders. We have lost the magic touch, gentlemen."

"Well, Padre," the engineer began, and paused, uncertain what had been said.

Reardon looked at them, and listened to the words go around. He watched Cortes at the bookshelf, turning the pages of a magazine. The room looked like it was arranged for a play, a drawing-room drama. They were all standing or sitting in threes, now silent. Reardon thought that someone had forgotten his lines. He sipped the beer and withdrew, watching.

"Señor Cortes works with us," Francis said to the engineer, leaning forward and pointing at Cortes with the beer can. "He is the government official who oversees the grants and loans. When we begin an irrigation or a model farm, Señor Cortes is the man we go to. He is the development man in Acopara."

"I see," the engineer said politely.

Cortes did not reply.

"Yes, the development man," Francis said.

"How much of that do you do here?" the engineer asked.

"As much as we can get away with . . . more sometimes."

"People have a right to run their own country," the engineer said, glancing at Cortes and smiling briefly.

"Sure," Francis said. "Except for the Indians."

"The Indians live," Cortes said.

"Well, they exist."

"Development of a poor country takes time," the engineer said.

"Depends on who's developing it," Francis said.

"There isn't growth overnight."

"Sure."

"It takes time."

"Right," Francis said, and sat down.

Reardon watched him, saw the thin smile sting his face and saw the eyes dip briefly. Now his bony body was stuck in the chair at right angles, and he looked a very old man. The talk slipped away, and Francis was left staring, holding the beer can with the pop-top. Father Peter Francis. He had two villains, American business and the American government, interchangeable parts. They were the predators, manipulators of interest rates and development loans, exploiters. For everything that was given, something was taken—usually something dear, priceless, like oil that lay under the land. He collected details of the piracy, and brought together the information and passed it on to friends in the capital. They would relay it, and print it in the leaflets that turned up here and there on the plain. That would tell the people what was happening. It was only a step from there to resistance.

Reardon watched Francis looking at Cortes, the easy-mannered bureaucrat. The talk had now definitely moved and slipped away. Francis was daydreaming again. He saw a bloodless transfer of power, a peaceful revolution in which the mission would essay a special role: moral leadership, a leadership drawing on the Christian ethic. He clung stubbornly to the idea, although all his readings in the history of the century taught him that moral leadership, whatever that was, was not enough. He faced the problem of direct involvement five years before, and after weeks at prayer decided against it. He could not be a party to killing, and would not advise others to kill. Old fashioned. He was very old fashioned. Do not ask anyone to do anything you are not willing to do yourself. That was how he defined responsibility. But the conditions were special, he told himself; Francis worked around it by giving money to men who asked him for it. He assumed the money went for guns, and the thought still hurt his conscience. He understood that he compromised, and worried about it every night and morning. He knew what he was doing, but could not do less and was incapable of doing more.

In his travels, Francis sought men to lead what he saw as a revolt, but he was disappointed. He traveled to the small towns on the plain, celebrating mass and talking quietly to anyone who would talk with him. What is life like here? he would ask. Who owns the land? Who are the officials? Who are the ones who go to school, and where? *Are there any leaflets?* He looked for the young men, but after two or three meetings they stayed away. Then Francis would learn they had left for the coast, the capital. Resist, he whispered; and they agreed, and nothing happened.

—We need money, Padre.

—Money.

—Not much. A little money.

There are no Gandhis anymore, Reardon told him brutally. Don't look for them, they don't exist anywhere. And don't belong on the plain if they did. One day he gave Francis a book of poems, the verse of Georg Herwegh,

> Until our hand turns to ashes,
> Shall it drop the sword?
> We have loved long enough.
> Now, finally, we wish to hate.

Francis, disappointed, placed his faith in students, but there were few of those in Acopara, and he worried that any rebellion would overlook the plain. The plain would be forgotten amid the urban disasters, which were real enough and more dramatic and received more attention. He talked about that in the small towns, talked without discrimination or understanding that they were watching him.

So one afternoon he was visited in the church by six young men, who cornered him and administered a quick and efficient beating. They found him in the small church in a town fifty miles from Acopara, and formed a circle and put Francis in the middle of it. They batted him back and forth like a medicine ball, slapping him with their open hands. Francis recalled later that the sound was like applause. None of them said anything. They slapped him from one side to the other, grabbing an arm or his neck, pushing and slapping him in the face, and finally battering him to the ground with their fists. When he tried to cry out, they stuffed cloth in his mouth. It was all done in fifteen minutes, and the six walked out of the church as wordlessly as they had walked into it. The beating left Francis nearly deaf in one ear, and he was more careful after that. He never learned who they were, but he supposed they had been sent by the provincial police. No one else would have reason to beat him so badly. The authorities promised to find those responsible, but they warned Francis that it was dangerous for him, for any gringo, to wander about unescorted in the small villages. Dangerous too, they said, to talk about politics. People did not understand; politics were a local affair.

But the old man persisted, believing that conditions could not stay the way they were, and that God would guide the people from the wilderness. No one was entirely forsaken. That was what he believed, and what he continued to preach. But he was more careful now, in what he said and who he said it to.

Meanwhile, until there was movement, he talked frankly in Deshais's apartment. He spoke of the American government and American business to anyone who would listen, even the hostiles—the fresh-faced engineer, for example; engineer or spy, whichever he was. They must know where he, Francis, stood.

The others were talking when Francis interrupted: "Government and business, one giant combine." He was looking at the engineer.

"But—for what purpose?" the engineer said after a moment.

"To control the lives of the people," Francis began, but stopped when Sister Marie leaned over and touched his arm and smiled.

"We baptize the young, and perform marriages, and that sort of thing," the sister said, her hand resting lightly on the priest's arm. "But it is very difficult in this country, which is so poor, as you know . . ."

"The Indians like the Christian ceremony," Brother Irwin said.

"They don't understand all of it, but they like it."

"It formalizes what has already taken place," the sister said slowly, talking straight at the engineer, looking at his face. "They have trial marriages here . . . so there are likely to be one or two children already from the marriages, before we formally come to marry them. Do you understand that?"

"I see," the engineer said. The sister and the old priest were looking at him, their heads side by side about a foot apart. A two-headed person, the engineer thought. Then Francis repeated what he had said before.

"To control and exploit. To control and exploit the Indians," he said. "Ask Señor Cortes. Cortes knows. Is that not right, señor?"

Cortes had replaced the magazine, and was standing stiffly, looking down at Francis, listening. Francis was grinning up at him, slowly sipping the beer.

"Right?" Francis demanded.

"The padre talks a great deal," Cortes said.

"So I see," said the engineer.

"Talk is cheap," said the old priest, tapping the beer can against his jawbone.

The sister began to speak, but Cortes cut her off. "No one controls the Indians," he said.

"Really?"

"Not even the government," said Cortes.

Then Deshais was in the room, introducing himself, pouring drinks, wrestling himself out of the surplice and laying it aside, explaining what it was that Sister Marie and Father Francis meant, talking of the *total mission*, the total responsibility of the missionary, the concern for stomachs as well as souls, the way of life. He gathered up all the loose ends, strand by strand, and led them in to lunch, where Cortes went to his left, the American engineer to his right.

The mestizo servant hustled, listening hard for the few English words he knew, the commands to clear the soup plates or to bring on the ice cream. The engineer was persistent in his questions, turning to talk to Deshais directly. What did Deshais think about the Indians?

"Oh, well, poor souls," Deshais said.

"Yes, but what can you *do?*"

"Well, we marry them and bury them."

"Yes."

"Be of use."

"To them?"

". . . and help them along, over life's little rough patches. Right, Father Francis?"

Francis grunted.

"They need you then?" the engineer asked.

"We need them more than they need us," Deshais said.

Chapter Three

ACOPARA WAS DESERTED when he stepped into the street. The others had gone back to the mission house, and Reardon could hear their voices trailing away. There was music somewhere, a Telefunken bringing the message from the capital. Behind him, the façade of the church loomed yellowly in the dark, above it the close-hanging stars and the cold. Reardon looked at the window, but lamps from the square cast shadows on it and its figures could not be seen in detail. It was a muddy and obscure black window. Thunder reached him from the mountains, faint but distinct. Present. The square was silent, its empty benches set like squatting animals under the trees. Someone, probably an Indian filled up with brandy, was lying on one of the benches, his head cradled in his arms and his legs played out over the edges. The square was Spanish, beautifully symmetrical, each building balanced by another, the church the keystone, dominant, holding it together. There was nothing in it to change, and anywhere else it would be a model square, a thing of classic beauty, architecture; in Acopara, it was the Plaza de Armas. Reardon paused at the square, then strolled across it and the street and walked up the alley, bound for the café. It was the only café in town open late at night.

He did not walk twenty paces when he abruptly changed his mind, turned about, and re-crossed the square. He wanted to look in at the radio station. There was no reason for it, except a desire to forget about the evening at Deshais's. Lunch lasted until four, and they had sat around the table talking until six. It was drinks time then and they drank until dinner and talked more after it. It was a long day leading to a longer night. Deshais's late nights were regretful things, long inquiries into the past, *his* past, and more; he wanted to forget about that. The radio building would be deserted now, at eleven o'clock; the programs ceased at nine, and the workers were gone five minutes later. Reardon walked the two blocks to the radio building, and let himself in with a key. The building was a white bungalow set back from the street, approached through a courtyard, low and dark with the tower hovering over it. Reardon noticed a faint red glow from the lights strung up the tower.

The entrance gave onto an auditorium, where the Indians came to listen to the programs. The place stank of dirt and stale urine. Reardon turned on the light, a bare bulb fastened to the ceiling, and looked about. The watchmen were gone. He shook his head and smiled, lit a cigarette and waited. It happened every time, every night after the programs. He walked slowly between the folding chairs to a small black bundle near the wall. He looked down at it, and very gently prodded it with his foot.

"Come on now."

The bundle stirred, and two black eyes looked at him.

"You can't stay here," he said in Spanish.

The eyes held his, unblinking.

"Come on, you've got to go home."

There was no response.

"You can't stay here."

The bundle moved again, and a small arm touched Reardon's leg.

"It's not allowed. Regulations."

It was a child, eight years old, perhaps twelve. The hand groped and finally took hold of Reardon's trouser cuff. The hand held, and jerked it.

"No, I'm serious."

"Cold," the child said softly.

The face was wrapped in a tattered blanket, and only eyes showed. The voice was soft and indistinct as cotton, a mumble coming from the darkness.

"Regulations," Reardon said in English.

The child stood and wrapped the blanket tightly around arms and body, shivering in the cold of the room, yawning, standing uncertainly. Where to go now?

Reardon watched, one leg up on a chair, his arms crossed on his knee, perched like a bird on one leg. One hand hung down and the smoke from the cigarette came up through his fingers and hung heavily in the room. The child's hair was black and matted, filthy, gummed together. "What the hell," Reardon said. "Stay where you are."

But the child was already walking away from him.

"Stay," he said in Spanish.

The child continued to walk toward the door, dragging the blanket.

"No, you can stay here, stay where you were. The hell with it," he said, not moving from the chair.

But the child was gone, out the door and into the cold.

Reardon called again, and moved to the door and looked out. The child was gone, vanished. She must have begun running as soon as she was out in the street. He flipped the cigarette into the gutter and went back into the building.

Reardon shook his head and walked to the front of the auditorium, a blank room in the dim light, suffused with shadows. He left the outside door open, thinking perhaps the child would come back; well, probably not. The kid was probably still running, running scared. He looked at the amplifier on the wall, and the two large windows that looked into the room from the places where the engineers played the records and the announcers talked about them. The Indians sat in the auditorium and watched the technicians through the glass.

Reardon passed through a side door and into the room that held the recordings, the rock records for the benefit and enjoyment of the technicians, and the traditional music that was played for the audience. There were almost five hundred records, mostly gifts from Catholics in the United States. They came in battered dust jackets with names and schools printed in black ink: *Jennifer O'Reilly, White Plains High School.* The USIA tapes gathered dust in a corner. On a lower shelf was the small collection of recorded Spanish lessons, lessons in perfect Castilian: the aristocratic lisp. For Madrid, say it *"Ma'rith."* Should an Indian find himself in Segovia or San Sebastian for the season, the accent would serve him well.

He ran his fingers along the edges of the recordings and went on out of the record room and into A Studio. One of the guards, a watchman, was lying on a couch, asleep. He was breathing softly, his chest hardly moving at all, and as Reardon came closer to him he could smell the brandy. There was no need to be quiet; equally, no need to wake him up. There were no thieves in Acopara, and no one to disturb the radio station. There was nothing to steal, except the records; and the technicians stole most of those. Well, Reardon reflected, he had taken one or two himself. There were some records that were unplayable on the high plain, some that did not translate. The guard shifted on the couch, and one hand tumbled off his crotch and struck the floor. His face did not move. Then he woke up.

"Go back to sleep," Reardon said.

"Señor, a small nap." His eyes were fuzzy and unfocused, and his voice thick. He was trying to remember who Reardon was.

"Never mind," Reardon said.

The guard was on his feet, unsteady. A gringo could not be an intruder.

"Go back to bed."

It sounded like an order, so the guard sat down again on the couch, holding his hands primly in front of him, as if he was gripping a small bouquet.

"Yes, señor."

"I will not be here long."

"Take all the time you want."

"I am just looking around."

The guard smiled. He was sleepy and the room was heavy with brandy fumes. He knew Reardon now as one of the Americans who had authority at the radio station. There were five or six

Americans who came in and out, and it was impossible to tell who was a priest and who was not. The guard called all of them *señor*.

Reardon paused at the door of the control room.

"Where is the other one?"

"The other one? Ah. His boy is very ill. He is at the infirmary with his son."

"So he is not here?"

"His boy has stomach sickness. It is very serious, señor. My friend was worried, and took him to the infirmary. It happened yesterday, and I believe . . ."

"He should let us know when he is not here."

"It was a very sudden illness."

"Tell him I am sorry."

"I will."

"Tell him if he needs help, to come to me."

"I will."

"Still, there should be two guards at the station."

"That is true enough. The equipment . . ."

"Anyone can see the dangers."

"Yes, señor."

Reardon nodded at the guard, and closed the door. The control room was sleek with metal, the dials gleaming in the bright light, the turntables large and fuzzy with felt. He looked out into the auditorium and thought he saw the bundle, up against the wall where it had been when he came in. But the light was so poor he could not be sure; there was a reflection from the control room glass. He put his face to the window and cupped his hands around his eyes. Perhaps it was just a shadow. Reardon smiled, and then he laughed. The depression of Deshais's was gone. He felt well, in among the machinery.

Reardon knew about radio stations, from a year in Boise after the murderous year in London that had followed the four murderous years in the monastery. In Idaho: long trips with a pack and a shotgun, and Boise itself, small and friendly, safe, quiet, uncomplicated. He was free then, without responsibilities, and with plenty of money—not that Reardon ever required very much. He hitched a ride to Boise after London, after he had come back to America. He signed on first as a ranch hand, then as a clerk in a dry goods store, finally as an announcer for a small radio station. The station in Acopara reminded him of the one in Boise: the equipment was similar, and the men were amateurs.

He ticked his thumbnail against the microphone. *This is Michael Reardon with the neeewz.* No one knew anything about radio announcing. It was an exacting art, far more exacting than its practitioners, even the best of them, were willing to admit. News came from the ticker and it was announced by a man sitting behind a glass wall in a soundproof room. It was announced as if it was something that had actually happened, rather than something you were reading. Ripped off the teletype, it read with urgency and sense, embellished by significant pauses. Reardon acquired a fascination for the troubles in Cyprus, then reaching a crescendo of blood, and the personage of President Makarios.

More troubles in Cyprus tonight. The United Press International reports the village of Ayios Sozomenos under seige by Greek Cypriot irregulars led by the resourceful Nikos Sampson. Five Turks dead, two wounded at last report. The President, Archbishop Makarios, is understood to be following these events in Nicosia . . .

He had made a study of the Cypriots, and knew the names of all the players. There was the stolid Turk, Fazil Kutchuk, and Kutchuk's associate, the ominous Rauf Denktash. There were others. The President's personal physician, Vasos Leserides, was one, and the fighting newspaper publisher, the gunslinging Nikos Sampson, another. Reardon fancied he could wring more syllables from the President, The Archbishop Makarios, than any radio announcer living or dead. Makarios was never "he"; when a synonym was required, that synonym was "His Beatitude." Transmitting the news over the radio was a way of life; it was, when you thought about it, some four shades removed from the reality, further even than newspapers or television, which Reardon concluded often *was* the reality, the central perception, a perception more crucial than the event itself. The teletype copy, yellow and perforated around its edges, hanging like tapestry beside the machine, was businesslike, relentlessly neutral, as objective as a multiplication table. Subject. Verb. Predicate. No room for misunderstanding. He caused the machine to be moved into the small studio where the news was announced, to give listeners a sense of rhythm, of the transmission of events, the clicking of the machine a counterpoint to the smoothness and authority of his voice. He cultivated that, too, a voice rich and baritone, knowledgable, a voice right down the middle, a voice like a smartly batted ball. For the evening newscast, he opened: *Ladies and gentlemen, good evening to you,* the first three words slow and deep, the last four slower still and tripping on the tongue. *Goooood ev-ening toyew.*

Of course it made no difference, because no one listened with care. His friend the station manager, a migrant from the East Coast, confided: "For there to be great poets, there must be great audiences." There were no audiences in Boise at seven A.M. and noon and five P.M. and nine P.M. In six months, Reardon received not a single fan letter; only at the bar down the street was he something of a celebrity, a man in direct and personal contact with . . . events. In Boise, Reardon read the news into the microphone and pretended he was talking to himself.

It went very well until one winter's night the radio station burned down and the news stopped. It ceased for five days until a new transmitter could be brought from Los Angeles. Then the citizens of Boise and its districts could learn again of the plans that President, The Archbishop Makarios, had for his country. Trappers and hunters, men who lived outside the cities, were then back again on the beam, in the mainstream. Cyprus was no longer isolated, but part of the life of Idaho. But by then Reardon was gone, gone without notice, leaving the management of the radio station to find someone else to read the news. He left the radio station to answer an advertisement: a traveling man offered one hundred dollars and expenses to drive a Buick from Boise to Miami, and did not care how long it took as long as the car was at the Eden Roc Hotel on November One. It was then October Five, so Reardon took the job. His radio career was ended.

He was looking at the control panel, inspecting the dials and switches, and remembering the journey, Boise to Miami in twenty-six days, observing the country from the windows of a sedan traveling at high speed. He kept his eye on the odometer, calculating distance one hill to another, watching the miles turn over, relentless as time. He was alone, and drove with his left foot on the dashboard, his right arm flung out across the thick seat cushions. South to Tucson, north again to Denver, east to Omaha, south to New Orleans, north to the Cumberland, then thirty hours straight to Florida, sleepless with music filling his head. An endurance, that uneven passage, carefully watching the signs, estimating America from its sights, speed limits, no left turns, *Yield,*

Merge, Eat, Gas, and *Jesus Saves.* The road straight, then turning, winding down through the mountains, and flat, deadly flat across Florida, flat as a book, the line in the center of the highway straight as a finger pointing to—Miami. Miamimiamimiamimi- amimiami. *You Are Now Entering The City Of Miami. Please Drive Carefully.* He did, and a year later he was in New York. The Cuban refugees and the hookers were left behind, and he took the voyage up the Eastern shelf by train. Luck. Luck brought him close to the Harris Foundation. Reardon looked at the controls of the transmitter, and through the glass into the auditorium. There was no auditorium in Boise.

Reardon walked to the wall, and pulled a heavy switch down: it sparked as the wires engaged, and the transmitter throbbed and began its hum, working perfectly (sometimes it didn't). Then he pushed two smaller toggle switches, moving them sideways on the control panel, and thumbed a button. When the button depressed, a red light appeared on the panel. The needle in the main dial bounced, and registered. Reardon smiled, set the dial, and leaned over the controls so his mouth was an inch away from the microphone.

This is the captain speaking.

Abandon ship.

Reardon was careful not to wake the guard on his way out. He closed the door quietly behind him, and fastened the padlock. The radio station was secure. He retraced his steps back to the plaza, and across it. The Indian was still lying on the bench, and the square was silent. It was as he had left it. He heard the noise of a car somewhere on the edge of town. Reardon stood still for a moment, looking at the empty streets and at the church, the dark window with the Rivera figures, the heavy door with its iron latch and sword-shaped hinges. Behind him were the high red lights of the radio tower, steady, very steady, warning aircraft.

He walked to the café, listening to the clicks his heels made on the pavement. He was across the square, preparing to enter the alley, when he turned and saw that the Indian on the bench had got up and was standing under a tree, watching him. The shadows fell across the Indian's face, and all he could see clearly was his body, feet wide apart, poncho wrapped tightly around his shoulders against the cold. Reardon shrugged and continued down the alley, but he had not gone a hundred feet when he heard the shuffle behind him. He crossed the alley, and looked around casually; the Indian was there, head bent, walking in a shuffle which was almost a stagger. The alley went on a hundred yards, then forked, and the café was on a street off the left fork.

Reardon walked on, more quickly now, conscious of the shuffle behind him. The doorways were dark and empty, the alley illuminated only by puddles of light near the square and the fork. He walked a little faster, to get out of the gloom, and he could tell from the noise behind him that the Indian was keeping pace. Reardon did not like the idea of forcing it with a drunk Indian in an alley at midnight. Possibly the Indian had mistaken him for a mestizo, because the gringos were out of bounds; Indians didn't tangle with gringos. But he was there, now twenty feet behind, and following, no question about that. Reardon stepped up the pace, his heels clicking and scraping the stones, trying to reach the light before he would turn and set himself. A drunk or drugged Indian was no one to run from. Then the shuffle stopped and Reardon walked on. He stood under the light and turned, and looked back into the dark of the alley. He saw the Indian standing there, motionless, standing in the shadows near a doorway. The two looked at each other. Reardon moved off to the left, and now the Indian was with him again. It was fifty yards down the left fork of the alley before the turning, and the café.

He was walking slowly now into the dark, both hands in his jacket pocket. The Indian was one of those from the fields, dressed in blue trousers and a heavy poncho, and a llama wool hat with earmuffs. Reardon saw enough of his face to know he was young, and very lean; the hat made his face longer and leaner, the light coming off the planes of his face, off the cheekbones and his forehead. The Indian looked mean as hell, Reardon thought, and would get meaner as it developed Reardon had very little money. He walked faster now and crossed the alley, and the Indian followed, gaining a bit Reardon thought, but still too far behind to rush. Only a few yards now to the turning, and the light of the café. The Indian was lagging a little, and the shuffle stopped when Reardon reached the tiny street. He turned again, but could not see the Indian. Probably he stopped in a doorway, to watch which way Reardon went. He had lost his chance, Reardon thought; botched it. His shoulders came loose again, and he took his hands out of his pockets. Neat. It was neatly done. He walked to the café and opened the door and went in.

Reardon took a table in the rear, greeted the owner, and ordered coffee and the local brandy, a liquor that tasted like anise and burned the mouth, then and later. The bored and tired owner nodded and slowly moved off behind the counter to fetch the drinks. Reardon was a regular customer after midnight, and now he wanted to tell the owner about the Indian. But he did not. The owner wouldn't believe him anyway; Indians didn't attack gringos, *claro*. It was an ill-lit and homely café, with a wooden bar and a dozen tables, and the smell of fried meat and beer. The owner kept cats, which padded over the tables and rubbed their backs against customers' legs. Tonight the café was empty except for five men sitting at another table, the one closest to the door. They were men from the fields, and were smoking and talking loudly in dialect and drinking beer. When Reardon entered, they lowered their voices and kept them lowered. They drank with their hats on, and after Reardon spoke to the owner one of them rose and went outside, slamming the door.

Reardon nursed the coffee, and toyed with his brandy glass. He was still nervous from the encounter, or near encounter, with the Indian. He quickly drank off one glass of brandy and ordered another, feeling in his pockets to make certain he had the money to pay for it. Probably the owner would put it on a tab; but you never knew. The owner had a fearsome wife. He relaxed in the chair, leaned back and put his feet out, hooking his ankles around the table legs. He could tell Deshais about the Indian tomorrow, and that would keep Deshais occupied for a week. It would give him something to talk to the officials about. *Mira, a desperate Indian*, Deshais would tell them; desperate Indians stalking the streets at night, menacing the innocent. There would be a report on the incident. Then Deshais would feel free to warn Reardon again that it was his own fault, that the mission house was the only safe place after dark. Cease prowling at night! At night, the streets belonged to the people.

Reardon sipped the brandy and forgot about the Indian. Goddam Deshais. It was an eighteen-month effort to get Reardon into the confessional, the late-night drinking confessional. Francis and Irwin had been there before him, but that was their business;

Irwin's story was too complicated anyway. Deshais was after facts, specifics, names and places and situations. The hell of it was that sometimes memories so filled his head that once or twice Deshais had nearly succeeded. Tonight was typical, a chipping away at the past. The past is prologue, is what Deshais went by. So leaning over the whisky bottle, hands clasped in his lap, the voice soft as a cat's paw: *Whatja do in London, Michael? Whyja go there?* And thinking about just that when he spoke, thinking about nothing else, concentrating only on memory . . . he nearly replied. Edward Deshais. Edward the Confessor.

Well, Padre, what do you do when you are out of a monastery on your own motion? Sprung from a hermitage. Why, rob banks. No? Four years in a monastery does not fit you for a trade, Padre; there is little you can do with what you have learned. See, Padre, *mira,* one was obliged to become a voluptuary. The Temptation of Reardon. You know (wink) how it is, Padre. Know what I mean?

The son of a bitch. So he started on the easiest first, the few verifiable facts that he had, the facts contained in the letter from Smyth and Donnelly and weasled away, ferreting, using his Edward the Confessor voice.

—Tell us about the monastery, Michael. How long was it? Five years? Six?

—Like most monasteries, Padre.

—How many years?

—Four years, more or less.

—In . . . Ohio, wasn't it?

—The Midwest.

—But . . . Ohio, I know that one, the one you were at. I visited that one once.

—Right.

—And then . . .

—Then.

—But?

—My glass is low, Padre.

—Oh, my, yes.

—Irish. I think I prefer the Irish.

—Yes, Irish is all right. Smoky, though. But it has the taste of the fields.

—Scotch hangovers are murder.

—Well, Irish . . .

Deshais had pieced together a little over eighteen months: place, length of time, not very much more. Deshais was divertable, almost to anything—to the virtues of Irish whisky over Scotch, to Vermont over New Hampshire, to St. Paul over Peter, Land-Rovers over jeeps. The list was endless, but he never stopped trying, never ceased trying to exhume the remains, a persistent and careful undertaker. Now it was a game. Well, Deshais was all right. Peter Francis also, and the rest of them. None of them liked the café, which was fine. The only one of them who would drink in the café was Bicker, and that turned out to be a mistake because Reardon told too much to Bicker over drinks; or not too much, but Bicker had no real interest, and what did it matter anyway. Bicker was gone now, a virtuous man, dealing holy cards to the rich in upstate New York. Acopara and the plain had virtues, and the padres were among the virtues.

Watch them in the chapel, in black, sitting stiff as crows in the pews, the Bible a part of them, a third hand. Who else cared, was willing to *risk*? With some of them, under the details lay something very like steel. The high plain under these circumstances did not diminish faith. Call them small saints, or maybe large ones.

One could not know the dimensions for some time, and perhaps would never know them. But watch them in the chapel.

Acopara was part of Reardon's life now, as much as the monastery had been and London after it, and Boise after that. Commuter traffic, he thought; waystations. And now, at this moment, it was a small and evil-smelling café with scarred tables and a surly proprietor; and the cats; and the five, no four, Indians at the table by the door. And the cold coming through the windows and the door when it was opened; and the regulars, the Indians, in from the fields to share a beer and a brandy. And on the hour in the daytime, the single tolling bell at the church; a reminder. He knew nuns and gas station attendants, one doctor, a bureaucrat and assorted other citizens. None of them came to the café.

He drank the coffee, then blotted out its taste with a sip of brandy. One's life ran in a straight line of routine. Tomorrow morning: holy cards. Tomorrow afternoon: the radio. It could be a fine radio station, as good in its way as the one in Boise, technically smart, if only there were sufficient receivers on the plain and additional power for the transmitter. Vital, he thought, a vital link. The station only reached a forty-mile radius, and there were blank spots in that, due to the mountains and the climate. Harris was to supply some new equipment, but New York was holding it up. Smyth and Donnelly were sitting on the papers in New York; they were probably in an in-box, ignored. The radio project did contain some hope, if you thought that bringing news into the lives of the Indians constituted a basis of hope. No, that was unfair. The radio could teach reading and writing. If the mission was able to arrange for more funds, either its own, Harris's, or the government's, there could be education over the entire high plain. But they needed ten thousand radios before the end of the year to make a decent start. Now there were three thousand and it was not enough, not nearly enough for a real program. That was what the permissions were all about. Reardon wanted the mission to control the money. The government seemed to want the radios distributed, but as always the money complicated the problem; it was a question of how much squeeze off the top the officials would require. There was no way to prevent a percentage, particularly in light of the latest report—that there would be a grant from the United States government. That was most puzzling of all. A conversation with the governor was unsatisfactory.

Reardon and Deshais went to see the governor one morning. They sat comfortably in his paneled office and drank coffee, Reardon pressing and Deshais nervous and conciliatory. Deshais did not want trouble. But the governor made it difficult to avoid.

The money must be spent by the state, he'd said; it was a government project, after all. The air was theirs. They could not permit foreigners to control a radio station on their own soil. A surrender of sovereignty, that. True?

Nodding vigorously, Deshais agreed. Absolutely. *Mira* . . .

The governor, speaking very smoothly and confidently, nodding now to Deshais, now to Reardon went on: "We cannot have foreigners controlling the apparatus of communications in Acopara and the plain, what with . . . conditions as they are. This must be done with the authority of the government." He said: "As one of your own wise men told us, 'control the communications and you control the society.'"

That bastard. Reardon remembered the look he had given Deshais, and the embarrassed smile he got in return. Deshais had looked at the governor and replied, sweetly: "That would be . . . ah, Mister Gaskell."

The governor agreed that it was.

What it meant was that the government would negotiate the contracts for the radios. Probably they would be Japanese radios, but if the money came from the American aid program the policy would be to buy American. In any case, the government would control the funds. Reardon had one last warning, which was delivered with no visible effect.

—So we turn the money over to you, and you will negotiate contracts for the radios.

—Correct.

—Our superiors in New York, both the padre's and mine, will want an accounting, Governor. A formality of course. But necessary for the American tax requirements. Mister Gaskell no doubt was ignorant of those. You understand.

—Certainly.

The governor had nodded and smiled, a secure man in the face of empty threats.

That was what was holding it up, the accounting procedures. Of course it would eventually go through. Graft was budgeted along with everything else. And the governor would get his fair share. The mission had worked on it for three years, and something always snarled. Money arrived and nothing happened; or money didn't arrive and nothing happened. Except six months ago it all came together at once, the money and the construction, and the radio station was built in sixty days. Even the army came to help with the tower.

Reardon drank the brandy and ordered another and thought: Everything was slow. Either the government demanded too much, or the people cooperated too little. One priest left and another came, and the project, whatever it was, languished until the new man caught on and understood it. Urgency was a self-defeating attitude, and always there were the tensions of the population. The mestizos thought the Indians were animals and the Indians thought the mestizos were exploiting them; when they thought about the mestizos at all. Then, in the middle of a project, something idiotic happened. The idiocies could be depended upon, like the afternoon rain in spring.

When the first radios were delivered, the first of the original shipment of three thousand, bought and paid for by the mission before the government got into it, an official of the United States Information Agency arrived with a bundle of tape recordings, which he offered free of charge to the mission. It was easier to accept them than to refuse them, so Deshais took them with thanks. Then it developed the Americans wanted to run a rating on the programs; they wanted a survey, to calculate which programs were popular and useful and which were not. Failing to make progress with Deshais, the USIA man came to Reardon about it.

—A small sample, a couple dozen families, no more.

—*Here?*

—Yes. Find out what the Indians like to listen to.

—Well, it is our experience that they turn the radios on in the morning and turn them off in the evening.

—But we want to know what they *listen* to.

—There is only one station, ours. When it is transmitting, they listen to it, all of it.

—But we are interested in which programs.

—All the programs.

—But they must listen to some programs more than others.

—I wouldn't count on it.

—Then we can find out.

—Do you speak the dialect?

—No.

—Do you know people who do?

—No. We thought we would hire them here. Hire local people. We have money to pay for this.

—Well, fine. I think it is an excellent idea.

—You'll help then.

—Sure. With pleasure. I can get you a dozen excellent interviewers, men who know the country, know the people, understand the technique.

—We wouldn't need more than six. It's a small sample we want.

—Oh, but it's a large plain, and transportation is difficult. People live spread out here. No, I'd say you'll need a dozen, maybe more, if what you want is a decent sample of opinion.

—The budget isn't large . . .

—That's all right.

—They'll all get a per diem.

—That's what I had in mind.

And employment, for two months, rose in Acopara.

Reardon smiled thinking about it. The survey, "the Nielsen" as Deshais called it, was better than a road or a dam or a canal, steadier work and the checks arrived on time. Reardon acted as agent, and for two months he was a popular man in Acopara. It became known that he had substantial funds at his disposal, a cornucopia by the standards of the town. His room at the mission was the unemployment center, and he and Deshais selected only the poorest and most wretched of the Indians who came to the mission. The mechanics of the survey kept them in laughter for weeks, until the embassy learned what was happening. Then the funds stopped.

The other missionaries felt there was something dishonest

about taking the money, but conceded that anything that helped unemployment was beneficial, a grace. Father Thomas and Brother Irwin led the opposition, complaining to Deshais that the mission should not become involved; repercussions were inevitable. No one wanted trouble. Father Francis objected on grounds that the mission should never, under any forseeable circumstances, have anything to do with the embassy; to treat with the embassy was to be an accomplice in its activities. But Deshais was taking delight in manufacturing the survey, inventing fractional numbers each night with Reardon, giving the educational programs enormous audiences. "Eight at night," he'd say, "prime time." The destitute Indians on the payroll of the American government never understood what they were meant to do, and reckoned the survey another obscure scheme by the foreigners in their midst. There were many such. For the Indians, it was one more bewildering episode in a series of bewildering episodes undertaken by the North Americans who unaccountably lived among them, enduring the height and the cold for no easily understandable reason. But every Friday night they went to Reardon's room and received wages, and handsome wages at that, more than they could earn in the fields or by begging in front of the church. *Lo peor es pedir,* the priest Deshais told them, but it made more sense, and seemed more truthful, when he had money to give them.

They did not know what to do about the missionaries, a dozen or so white men and women responsible only to God and to the authorities in America, who lived apart in compounds where they spent the evening hours. And Reardon, Reardon unaccountable too, a man who traveled in an automobile and asked questions connected with the construction of things, irrigation projects, radio stations, model farms. He carried holy cards, and was not a priest, had money, and chose to live in Acopara. On the rare, very rare, occasions when the Indians spoke among themselves of The Foreigners, they used a virtually untranslatable word. Reardon learned later that it meant, roughly, "others." Those who stood apart.

Well, he thought, how could you fault them? Deshais, Thomas, Francis, and the rest. Bicker. They demanded nothing for themselves, and took only what the plain could give them. And who knew about that, perhaps it was just another tree crashing in a distant forest. The Foundation? Bits and pieces of conscience balm and tax write-off—a model farm, a mighty dam, a microphone, brought to you by a lipstick company.

Fine, fine.

It was nearly one o'clock and the proprietor wanted to lock up. Reardon finished the last of his brandy and coffee, and made as if to go, thinking he would buy a bottle and take it with him. But there was an argument at the table near the door, and he saw one of the five men looking at him. The one who seemed to be the leader was talking roughly to the proprietor, and the proprietor was talking back. But he was not prepared to argue for long with five Indians who had been drinking. He collected the coins on the table, fired a last sentence at the Indians, and went back behind the bar to his living quarters.

Reardon watched one of them light a cigar and rise and approach his table. The Indian asked in broken English if he could sit. Reardon nodded, pulled out the other chair, and glanced over to the bar to signal for two more brandies. But the owner had left for good; the door was closed. The other men pushed back their chairs, two went outside, and two came to stand by the other.

"My name is Reardon," he said.

But the Indians knew who Reardon was.

Chapter Four

THE INDIAN MARTINEZ went first, Reardon second, and the others came on behind. They walked through the dark streets to the edge of town, where the horses were tethered behind a house. The conversation in the café was brief: the Indian said he had a sick wife who needed medicine. Reardon replied he was not a doctor. The Indian said it was not a complicated sickness, and Reardon said any sickness was too complicated for him. They drank a brandy and talked about it. Then the Indian said it was vital, necessary for Reardon to accompany them. There were six of them now. The Indian's Spanish was very bad.

The route was north, over the bridge and the hill outside of town, then higher onto the plateau and into the mountains. It took one hour to traverse the hill, moving slowly with the horses up one angle, then reversing and slowly climbing the other. It was cold and dark, and Reardon could see the hot breath of the horses as they labored. The men did not speak, and the only sounds were the clip of horses hooves, the movements of a stone, and the squeak of leather. Martinez had handed Reardon a poncho, and he wrapped it around his head and neck for warmth. They were only thirty minutes out of town, well before sunrise, when at a signal from Martinez the men unstrapped the packs on the rumps of the horses and extracted canvas gun cases.

The men balanced themselves in the saddle, belly forward, as they pulled the canvas away. About half the guns were blunt-nosed Sten automatics. The rest were shotguns, and the men were forced to drop reins as they worked to fit the flanges of the metal together, marrying the barrel and the breech on the wooden butt. All the guns had worn, leather slings. His horse moving away from him, one of the men lost his balance and the barrel clattered to the ground; the noise was loud in the night, and Martinez reined in and waited impatiently for him to dismount and assemble the weapon. Martinez's eyes moved along the rocks and to the summit of the hill, to the left and right there, and down the slope. He muttered a few short words to the one on the ground with the shotgun, and then they started again.

Reardon sat stiffly on his mount, looking at the party. There were six men, all of them young and one of them very young. They paid no attention to him except for the boy, who playfully fingered the trigger on his shotgun and adopted a set expression; mean, it said, very mean. *Don't tread on me,* Reardon thought, and felt old. It reminded him of the tough kids in school, the ones who swaggered, all elbows. The men were neat and quiet now, strung out behind Martinez in file; the boy came up behind Reardon, close enough to touch, holding the shotgun low by its

breech. It was for show, Reardon thought; to establish some atmosphere, draw the boundaries. But there was no need to take
out the guns so close to town. They did it for effect, and for whatever feeling it gave them to sling a Sten.

The path went up and over the high hill, and through a defile in
the abrupt range beyond. Below they could see the trail, and the
bridge and the shimmering ribbon of water flowing beneath it.
Ahead was the plateau, rising into the blackness of the earth and
the night. It was a part of the wilderness that Reardon had never
visited; his route was in the opposite direction, near the ruins. The
land was used now; desolate, a wasteland, but somehow occupied, if not by people by history. The trail was carved out of the
earth in the sixteenth century, when the Indians had a civilization
and were undisturbed. Every road or highway or aqueduct in this
part of the country was four centuries old, or the foundations
were. There is your economic infrastructure, Padre; the economic
take-off point of the sixteenth century. It was built and maintained
and used by the Indians until one Spaniard came with 180 men
and beat them, snuffed out a nation of 100,000 (or was it 3,000?
30,000? 130,000?) with 180 soldiers and gunpowder. He had help
from the Indians, who thought the Sun God was theirs and would
protect them; the Indians also counted on their priests, who were
powerful as well as wise. But the Sun God went with the Spaniard
and the priests defected; the nation split, and the Spaniard picked
up the pieces. He picked up all the gold and sent it back to Seville.
With God and the battalions, Europe won. Gunpowder won it for
them, and permitted the destruction of a civilization. They kept
the Spaniard's bones in a crypt in the capital, regarding him as a
national hero and world adventurer, much-admired deliverer of
the Spanish people, protector of the empire, and schoolchildren

came to admire the corpse. North Americans learned his name along with Vasco da Gama and Ponce de Leon, Magellan, and some of the others: de Soto. It was called the age of exploration. The Spanish influence hung on in the country, propagated by the church and its missionaries, and a trace of Spanish blood in the twentieth century was a mark of distinction, like being a Bradford of Massachusetts. Of course there was no Indian blood that anyone could trace, nor an Indian history or a civilization. North American scholars pored over the ruins and evolved theories. But no one else was interested. The only link from then to now was the land, and the Indians who lived on it.

Once in five miles the riders encountered a house, black in the distance but up close lit by a flickering candle or a peat fire, muted voices inside. The people did not look from their houses when the horses passed. All the faces were turned inwards, toward the walls or the fire. They sat quietly inside, chewing coca leaves and dreaming, or drinking from the brandy bottle. From time to time, Martinez would look inside the huts, and bend to wave a greeting and speak softly. The others kept their guns out of sight. The inhabitants did not seem to notice Reardon, who in the darkness passed for another traveler; except alone among the men on horseback, he had no gun.

There were buzzards now, barely seen in the dark, three of them looping in circles overhead, keeping just in front of the file of horses, their wings motionless, heads tucked down like swimmers' heads, black bodies suspended on wires. The birds tilted and came off, tilted and swung round again. Reardon watched them, dim ghosts, black ghosts watching the trail, circling, keeping company. The men began to talk among themselves in low whispers. Reardon's questions to Martinez were answered in surly monosyllables and shrugs, the voice barely audible. Three nights on the trail, he said; all was well, keep tranquil. The line of men and horses moved deeper into the mountains, always moving to higher ground, then traversing a valley, rising higher. They skirted two tiny pueblos and one white-washed hacienda, large and white in the darkness, with goats spread around it like sentinels. They passed herds of llamas tended by youngsters, although there was no place for the llamas to go in the darkness. The llamas watched the procession of men with curiosity and no fear, looking down at them with the haughty and amused expression of society ladies everywhere. The land was wild and beautiful, the plateau level as a rug with great escarpments exploding up and falling off into deep, green-bottomed valleys; when the moon came from behind clouds, it washed the plateau with a milky light, casting deep shadows below the rocks. The vegetation was scrub, almost more mineral than plant, that grew and moved in the wind like seaweed. It was walking on the bottom of the ocean, with buzzards as fish, the wind as waves and tide. The men rode for four hours before dawn came.

At first light, Martinez moved the horses into a trot. They broke off the trail toward a deep ravine and reined in at its edge. Martinez dismounted and ordered Reardon to follow. He carefully led his horses over the lip and down into the ravine, descending on a narrow trail, Reardon behind him and the others following. Fifty yards down, the trail ended at a cave whose opening was wide and high enough to permit a man and a horse to enter. The cave was as large as a banquet hall, formed into a foyer and two large rooms off it. The horses were led to one side, and the men gathered at the other. Without speaking, they broke open sacks of food. Water was available from a cache of canteens laid in one corner next to cartons of 9 mm. Sten clips. Martinez took off one of the packs of food, settled himself on a bedroll, and broke off sausage and bread and poured a cup of water, and handed them to Reardon. He told Reardon they would stay in the cave until nightfall. He was not to leave it for any reason; if he had to take a piss, one of the other men would accompany him. Martinez looked at Reardon and laughed: you are the one they will be looking for now, the missing gringo. He laughed with a mouth full of sausage and bread. At dusk, he said, the march would resume.

Reardon accepted the food and relaxed, his back against the cave wall. The men lit cigarettes, and these glowed in the half-light of dawn. Across from Reardon, the young Indian sat cross-legged, a Sten cradled in his arms. One thing about a Sten, Reardon thought, is that it is good for only one purpose. It was a badge of a killer as surely as a black mask at a gallows. The gun had no other purpose. It was cheap, easily produced, and inaccurate at a distance. It was not an instrument of precision. It discharged easily and was an altogether unreliable friend. The boy-killer looking at him did not seem too dangerous, but there was something odd about the face. Perhaps it was the hat. Then Reardon smiled. It was the alley Indian, the one who followed from the plaza.

"You like the Sten?"

The boy smiled thinly at Reardon's English, and toyed with the safety catch.

"Great gun; keep it with you."

The Indian smiled again, crookedly this time, and hefted the gun. One of the other men had given it to him. His own shotgun was propped up against the wall of the cave.

"Wonderful things, Stens. Keep it pointed the other way, comrade. It wouldn't do to have it go off. It wouldn't do at all, and I doubt if you know how to handle it, huh? The safety is near the trigger, friend."

The Indian turned to Martinez and said something in dialect, and Martinez looked back at Reardon. He walked to where Reardon was sitting and told him not to talk English again. It made the boy nervous.

"He doesn't understand Spanish," Reardon said.

"Then don't talk at all. Don't say anything."

Reardon looked up at Martinez, finished the sausage and bread, and water, and slept.

They rode for four nights, not three, Martinez repeatedly consulting a compass. Now there were fewer villages and fewer people, and the country grew wilder. All of it was wilderness, wolves at night and wild goats during the day. Discipline slipped, and the men began to smoke and talk carelessly. At night, moving across the tundra, Reardon dismissed all of them from his mind and concentrated on the high horizon, the stars and the mountains. There were glaciers in the mountains, and many of the valleys had never been explored; that is, white men had never been in them. Neither North Americans nor Europeans had been in them to take pictures, and bring back accounts; that is what discovery means. Reardon did not care where he was going, and did not care where he had been. At night the plain stretched off limitlessly, pulled to the extremity, the mountains going on as far as he could go, and beyond it. However far he could go, they could go farther and keep going.

Behind Reardon, the men murmured in dialect and occasionally laughed very quietly. For a time, they joked and amused each other, trying to stifle laughter. The jokes were very brief, thirty-second stories, and the men rocked back, their mouths baying, hilarious, pointing at the story-teller. Then they began a competition, to twirl the heavy Stens like American Western heroes twirled six-guns. One of them had got the trick, and the others looked at him in admiration until he banged the gun accidentally against the withers of his horse, which snorted and shuddered in pain, bringing a swift rebuke from Martinez. The Indian leaned down and spoke some words softly, and cradling the gun, stroked the horse's neck, talking to it like a woman. The men resumed talking quietly among themselves, the boy still behind Reardon, close enough to touch.

A rider came at dusk on the fourth day and guided them to the camp. At midnight they arrived at a collection of huts at the base of a hill, the huts built beautifully into the stone to blend with the terrain. The outlines of the camp only became visible a few yards away, as the horses approached the ridge line. It overlooked a valley and a stream dammed into a pond. Reardon saw it all by moonlight. He was left outside while Martinez passed through the entrance of the largest hut, bending and pushing aside a canvas cover. The men dismounted and began walking, stretching their legs. It was cold and pitch-black, and Reardon shivered in the saddle. Presently, Martinez came to the entrance and motioned Reardon inside.

He blinked in the light of the kerosene lamp, and followed Martinez to a small table where a man was bent writing into a ledger. He was hunched over the paper and scowling, printing with a cramped script very slowly, as if writing were an effort. There were benches along the walls and a map, and in one corner a dozen ammunition boxes; there was a fire in the corner and Reardon walked over to it and warmed his hands, feeling Martinez's eyes on his back. The windows were covered with black cloth. Cigarette ends and ashes overflowed a cup on the table. Reardon rubbed his hands in front of the fire, and came back to the desk. It was an effort to pull away from the warmth of the fire.

The man who was writing looked up and stared, holding Reardon's eyes for a long minute. He was like any of the Indians at the Plaza de Armas or in the café near the radio station, a nondescript man, medium height, medium build, forty-five years old, perhaps a bit older; a man of indeterminate age. Lines ran down the flat planes of his cheeks, the eyes deep-set, hard and fatigued. The years showed in the thick hands and the face, and the way he moved. He greeted Reardon with a weary expression of welcome, rising.

"Pacheco," he mumbled, and stuck out his hand.

It was meant to be a name, and Reardon smiled. "Pacheco" was the equivalent of Smith or Brown. Joe Smith at his service. He waited.

Martinez said something in dialect, and the older man nodded.

"They found you at the café?" he said in Spanish.

"Drinking brandy," Reardon said.

"You were?"

"I was. They were drinking beer."

Pacheco asked him if the journey was difficult or too boring. Was there sufficient food, water? "Martinez treated you well?"

"Fine. But it was cold."

"Well, there is some brandy here."

The *jefe,* the leader, spoke fluently and swiftly in Spanish, his voice deep and often lisping. Reardon was tired from the ride and found it difficult to focus his eyes. The lamp cast sharp shadows in the room, and every time the Indian moved, a bearlike image crawled across the wall.

"Warm yourself," he said, and the two walked to the fireplace. Reardon shucked the heavy poncho, and tossed it in the corner. The cold slowly left his face and his limbs. He wondered how anybody could live on the plain, could survive twenty-four hours a day in the cold. It did not seem to bother Pacheco, who wore only a battered army jacket and patched woolen trousers. Reardon looked up from the flames to the map, and stood staring at it. It was a map of the district, framed like a picture and set against the wall. There were pins in it, giving the map the aspect of a military campaign. Reardon looked at it and could not figure out where he was, or the location of Acopara. He regretted not knowing the terrain, not knowing the angle of the border or the location of the small towns away from the district.

Pacheco smiled. "This map is a souvenir from my army days. When I left the army three years ago, I took a pistol and this map. And some money. The pistol has disappeared, but the map is still there. It is not a very accurate map, but it is what the army uses. Acopara is off of it, down here"—he pointed to the floor, down and to the left of the map—"and the border is there."

"We are about a hundred miles from Acopara?"

The Indian nodded noncommitally.

Reardon stepped to the map and peered at it. "You are beginning World War Three?" He did not know what to call the Indian—Pacheco, Smith, would not do—so he added, "Colonel."

"A small part of it."

Reardon was looking at the map. He smiled and drawled in Spanish, dragging the sentences out. "Where are the artillery batteries? Where is the airfield? The secondary command posts? Where are the lines? Surely the lines have been drawn. I see no division insignia on this map, Colonel, nor order of battle. Where is the enemy?"

"All in good time, señor. World War Three will take time."

The colonel called for glasses and a bottle, and they began the preliminaries seated at opposite ends of the table, the bottle between them and the lamplight dancing on the walls.

Cold; it was cold. Yes, cold even in the hut, even with the fire. Firewood was low. Take another poncho, señor Reardon; it will become colder still before dawn. A comfortable headquarters, Colonel. Yes, señor; it is all right. But odd, there are no photographs; how odd, Reardon said. Photographs? Well, Ché, Fidel, Mao. Cautious laughter. No, it is a working headquarters, not a seminar or a classroom; not a café, either. You understand it, señor: although all of us carry in our hearts the saints of the revolution, those who have preceded us in battle, they are no use to us . . . here. They are there, like scars, with us all the while. Of course. Doubtless. Well, the colonel's Spanish is excellent, bearing no trace of either the Indian patois or the psuedo-Castilian spoken in the capital. Well, yes, señor, thank you for the compliment. Spanish is the language of the country, you know; some of us speak it well. It is a pity you do not know the Indian language, more colorful, less precise, which is often useful. The colonel, Pacheco, was complimented on his camouflage, the deportment of his men, the diligence of Martinez, his own disguise: Smith. Reardon, the gringo, was praised for his calm, for his tranquility, in what must be, yes, puzzling circumstances. They went back and forth, fenced around it for half an hour.

"Now that you are here," the colonel said, speaking as if Reardon had happened to drop in for the afternoon. "Now that you are here, we may have a job for you."

"A job?"

"Yes, señor. A job."

"Thank you. I appreciate the offer. But I have a job."

"A better one," the colonel smiled. "This is a better job."

"Ah. You want an American adviser, Colonel."

"Not exactly."

"Someone who understands the land."

"Not quite."

"The people?"

"No."

"An expert in munitions. Surely that's it."

Reardon was smiling widely, but the colonel was silent, lighting a cigarette.

"It is surprising," Reardon said, phrasing the sentences in elaborate, formal Spanish. "We have done beautifully wherever we have gone. I cannot understand why you would not want us. Perhaps we can do for you what we have done for the Asians. Perhaps I can finance you a fortress, or find a priest to serve communion in the trenches, on the barricades. There are no atheists on barricades, Colonel. You may know what a superb job we have done on the plain with the Indians, my friends in the mission and me. We Americans are experts in the guerrilla, and I cannot understand your attitude."

The colonel looked at him closely, with a tight smile. He was trying to make up his mind how to reply. Finally he shrugged, and poured another glass of brandy. "That will never happen," he said, shaking his head. "Not with you or with anyone else. No. American advisers are as wonderful as the plague."

"I am glad you see it that way, Colonel."

"That is the way I see it, señor."

He took a small map that was tucked into the ledger and laid it flat on the table. He motioned Reardon to come around next to him. Martinez was still at the door. "We have certain problems . . . they have plagued us for some time, making it difficult . . ." He let the thought hang, speaking casually. The colonel had not wanted to get into it so quickly. But gringos never spent time talking, preparing the ground. They were there right away, without preliminaries or amenities. Reardon's brandy was almost untouched. The colonel thought it an odd manner, and did not understand it.

The map was of Acopara district, drawn by hand, with the town in detail in the center. The road was marked in black pencil, and there were tiny checks and the church, the administration building, and the garrison at the edge of town. Around the radio station was a thick black circle. Reardon looked at it a minute and saw that the proportions were wrong. The map had been drawn from memory by someone whose recollections were very poor. It was a suicidal map, if the objective was to act on it.

"We want the radio station," the colonel said quietly, looking at Reardon.

"So," he said. "A broadcast."

"Correct."

"A quick raid," Reardon said, and the colonel nodded. "A broadcast. In and out."

"Yes."

"You won't get it with this map," Reardon said. "It's a terrible map."

"We do not have regular maps, friend. Neither do we have draftsmen. You will be interested to know we do not have doctors, either. Nor supply officers, nor ordnance officers, nor color bearers, nor colonels. We have twelve men, give or take a few, not a regiment."

"The map is not good, Colonel. The proportions are wrong. You drew it?"

"No."

"Whoever did does not know Acopara."

"He was born in Acopara, señor. He knows Acopara *much better* than you do. But he does not draw. He does not read or write. He handles a gun, not a pen. Understand?"

Reardon shrugged. "I am sorry about that, Colonel. But the map is no good."

The two stood in silence a moment, hunched over the table in the poor light, the colonel marking the major points on the map with his pencil, quick checks to emphasize what he said to Reardon: "You draw us a better one, señor. If it offends you, draw us a better one. We will be glad to have it. Pay particular attention to the radio station, the hills to the north and east, and their relationship to the garrison. We know all that from memory ourselves, but it will not hurt to have it down on paper. You can also tell us the routine of the guards at the radio . . ."

"They sleep," Reardon muttered.

". . . who they are and when they change, their armament, who commands them, how attentive they are . . ."

"They sleep," Reardon said.

"Good. You can tell us the hours when the Americans are there, and how many Americans have access to it. Most important, you can tell us how to broadcast. Once we are inside, we must know how to broadcast. We must have someone there to switch on the transmitter. We must know how to speak, how to know when the transmitter is working . . ."

"I'm glad you don't want much," Reardon said, smiling, listening carefully.

"The point of this operation, señor, is not to fire a shot. If there is any shooting, the operation is a failure. Because if there is shooting, I will be unable to broadcast, or will die in the attempt. Either way, a failure, no? We do not want to kill anybody, either Americans or anybody else—for no other reason, understand, than there is no need. More than that, we do not wish to be killed ourselves. There are not enough of us for . . . gestures, señor. We must take the station at a time when people are listening, when the radios on the plain are turned on . . . "

Reardon wasn't following it now. He took a long drink of the brandy, and shook his head to clear his eyes. Exhausted, he slumped in the chair, the light wavering in front of his face. He scarcely heard the colonel, but he felt the brandy go down, burning his throat and his stomach, warming his body.

" . . . and I think that is early in the morning. It is impossible during the day, and useless in the middle of the night. You see the problem?"

"It is a problem all right," Reardon said.

"I knew you would see it," the colonel said dryly.

"But why should I do anything about it?"

"What?"

"Why should I help?" Reardon said listlessly.

"There are a good many reasons, señor. It is not necessary to list all of them. You make up your own list. We are going to take the radio station. We can do it with great loss of life, or with very little. But we will make the attempt. If we must shoot, it means there can be no broadcast; or a limited one, very quick. And we have failed. Although in the process we may kill a few infantry. We can be successful or unsuccessful; we will try it nonetheless. Some of the obvious things you already know."

"Right," Reardon said. He felt worse, and he gripped the sides of the chair and tried again to focus. The brandy burned its way into his gut, and he took another glass. Tired. Too damn tired. Now was not the time for argument.

"You know that there are only about, oh, three thousand radios on the plain?"

The colonel didn't answer.

"And of those, you have got to calculate which will be on, turned on, *before* the station begins its regular broadcast. There will be a few. No one knows how many, and of those that are on—how many are being listened to?"

The colonel offered Reardon a cigarette and sat down heavily, spreading his hands wide, palms down on the table top. He glanced quickly at Martinez, and then he folded the small map and put it to one side. He hadn't listened to the statistics. He thought it was very tricky now, what to say to the American, strangely accommodating behind a mask of a face. Reardon showed no surprise at being where he was, had not demanded release or explanations; he had not complained or (the colonel smiled) insisted on telephoning the American consul. What he said about the map was true. It had been a very great risk bringing him to this place, a risk only outweighed by the risk of not having him at all, not having someone who understood the radio and how it worked, who knew the interior of the building and which switches to pull. It did not matter about the American, who could be killed tonight or in the morning; but the colonel did not trust himself or Martinez with radio switches. The colonel, looking carefully into Reardon's face, was trying to read what he saw there.

"I am not . . ." Reardon began.

"I know," the colonel said.

". . . a soldier."

"Forget that. We have the soldiers."

"With shotguns," Reardon smiled, and pointed at Martinez in the doorway. "And Stens. Some army. Stens: no profit there, Colonel."

The other looked at him evenly, not answering.

Reardon fought fatigue, and now his head was better.

"There is a garrison of troops in Acopara."

"I know that."

"And you have twelve men."

"With shotguns and Stens," the colonel mimicked.

"And there are three thousand radios on the plain."

"Everyone in this country will know about it the morning after, señor. Everyone."

"Yeh, I suppose." Reardon sat back and thought. "One question, *Jefe*. Why an American? There are Indians and mestizos who work in that radio station. Why not one of them? Why me?"

The colonel smiled, and drank off the last of the brandy. He wondered how to explain that. You tried in a dozen ways to move from the inside. The mestizos were useless, untrustworthy, and possibly treacherous. So on successive nights you visited the Indians, two terrified men who lived in the barrios with their families. You put it to them, what you wanted to do, and why you needed their help. First you put it gently and then not so gently. They begged off. They had families, and the families would come under suspicion. They would be the first ones questioned. They would be taken to the garrison and beaten, and when guilt was beaten out of them they would be thrown in prison. No, *Jefe*, you must find someone else; we can draw you maps, but that is all we can do.

The Indians were washed out: they were frightened men, and

after the colonel saw them he knew that he could force them into complicity, force them perhaps to draw the most detailed of diagrams; but they were dangerous men to have around, dangerous to have knowledge of the plans. What it meant was that the guerrilla could not work from the inside, at least not with the Indians. And at the end he was forced to threaten them to keep silence; the colonel told the Indians he would kill their families if they talked. He meant it, and they knew he meant it. He was forced to say that to one of his own. The colonel said to Reardon: "There were complications."

"I can believe it," Reardon said, and looked again at the map. He did not know precisely what they wanted him to do. But they could not get their own people, that much was clear; they had to go outside, to an American. It was pathetic, really; it meant more danger for them, and it meant further there was no support in the town, or on the plain. Anyway, it had nothing to do with maps. Anyone can draw a map. Martinez could draw one.

The colonel looked quizzically at Reardon.

"What do you know about weapons, señor? A man of your trade should not know about weapons, Stens. Where did you hear of Stens? A man of your background." The colonel turned to Martinez, who was still standing motionless at the entrance to the hut. "Juanito, the gringo knows all about weapons. Wonderful, eh?" A flicker of a smile passed over Martinez's mouth. He was slouched against the wall, listening sullenly to the talk.

"Yes, *Jefe*," Martinez said.

"It is an old hobby, Colonel. I know enough to know that yours are old, and probably half do not fire properly. A Sten is a bad weapon, except for the streets . . . "

"There is nothing wrong with these Stens, señor."

"If you like Stens."

"We will soon have new weapons," the colonel mumbled.

"Where? From where?"

The colonel paused, lost in thought. He looked at Reardon from behind the desk. "It does not matter where they are coming from," he said. "What matters is that they *are* coming, promised."

"Czechoslovakia?" he asked.

The colonel shook his head, puzzled; no, not Czechoslovakia.

"Cuba, perhaps?"

Smiling: "Cuba does not stand aside."

"But I understood you had Thompsons?"

"One Thompson," the colonel said. "And a Browning."

"I think you should make an effort to find some Czech weapons," Reardon said. "I think they would be very helpful."

The colonel looked at him blankly.

"If they find a Czech weapon, or a weapon from any of the European Communist countries, they will take it for granted that a major revolution is happening. I recommend a small plaque on each gun, 'This is a Czech weapon.' Of course a Chinese weapon would be even better. Much better, in fact."

Czech weapons, Reardon thought; the single enduring cliché of guerrillas everywhere. If they received Czech weapons and one fell into the hands of the enemy, there would be an American division on the high plain in a week. Reardon was suddenly enjoying himself.

"The Americans are very serious about Communist arms," he said.

The colonel looked at him blankly.

"If they find a Czech weapon here, they will assume a major revolution . . ."

The colonel shrugged, impatient.

"It might be a good idea to let one fall, let it be found by the enemy," Reardon mused. "It would do you more good than all the broadcasts you could make from now until . . . Christmas. Listen: you don't know the mentality of the Americans. It would be a wonderful thing to see."

The colonel wasn't following him. The arms were important, and he did not have them. They had been promised, a dozen times promised, but something always happened to delay the shipments. The communications were rotten. But when they got the arms, when the shipment finally got through, there was no point in deliberately giving one gun away to the government. The colonel frowned. The gringo was talking in circles, amusing himself.

"The point of it is propaganda, no?"

"Señor, we are making a revolution, not propaganda."

"Yes, but . . ." Reardon saw that the colonel was not with him, so he gave it up. But the idea was wonderful, and the seeds were there to destroy Gaskell. How was it possible to describe Gaskell to this guerrilla; it couldn't be done.

"What do they say about us in Acopara?"

"Very little," Reardon said. "That's the truth."

"You. Have you heard of us?"

"Rumors, Colonel. Nothing but rumors, and those very vague. There was talk of one prisoner, captured carrying a Thompson. Nothing much else. Was it true about the prisoner?"

"They have not captured the Thompson," the colonel said. "It was destroyed."

"A prisoner?"

"No prisoners."

"The Americans have done a study on the high plain, and the chances of a revolution."

"Study?" The colonel was puzzled. Reardon groped for the proper Spanish words.

"The Americans sent a . . . researcher, a scholar, a . . . ah, professor to Acopara to report on the guerrilla and the revolution."

"And what did the professor say?"

"He said there was a very serious problem on the plain. He said the guerrilla was strong, and getting stronger. He said the people were behind you. He said that the guerrilla was so"—groping again—"tight, secret, that no one knew the name of the leader. No one knows your name, Colonel."

"Good." He nodded. "Very good."

Reardon thought that he was not communicating Gaskell's true flavor. He went on: "The Americans believed the professor. The army received guns from the Americans, after the garrison commander swore to an American colonel that there was a guerrilla in the mountains. But the army offered no evidence, and no one took him seriously except the Americans. The army just wanted the guns."

"The Americans believed him, you say. Why not the others?"

Reardon laughed. "No evidence, Colonel. You cannot have a revolution without evidence. 'The objective conditions for revolution do not exist on the high plain.' Everyone says so. You know it."

"True, señor. True. But now it is only a beginning. The objective conditions must create themselves objectively." The gringo was amusing himself again, the colonel thought. "Objective conditions of revolution." It was an irony, more crap from the café rebels. There was no place in the world where the objective conditions were more correct, as they liked to say in the books, than on the high plain; and yet there was no revolution. Two and two did not make four. It only made twelve: twelve men, some shotguns and some Stens. Explain that, comrade. The only one of them who made any sense was Debray, and Debray not all the time. They talked of fronts and fists. The guerrilla was the armed fist of the revolutionary front, according to Debray; true, true enough, but so what? Well, at least the Frenchman had been there, knew firsthand what he was talking about, was not fully ignorant as some of the others were. The colonel had read a little of what Debray had published, and once had almost met him; it was when Debray and Guevara were in Bolivia. But Ché was dead and the Frenchman was in prison and now there were only words left behind, words leading to expectations. There was an idea that a continent was in rebellion, workers and students joined together, locked arms to throw out the oligarchy. Shit. The students were reading the Frenchman and writing songs about the Argentinian, and the workers were counting their pennies and worried about food. The armed fist of the revolutionary front. The armed front of the revolutionary fist. Take it either way, mister; you are welcome to it.

Two years ago, the colonel had met with Guevara, talked with him for an afternoon. But it was not successful. Guevara was remote, preoccupied with his own difficulties in Peru and Bolivia. He listened without interest to the problems of the high plain. They drank coffee and discussed the peasants, and the problems of communication. Guevara was fascinated with a new radio, manufactured in the United States, which was light and very powerful. He had all the details, as well as an instruction manual, and went over the radio fact by fact. That was what the colonel liked about Guevara: he dealt in facts, details. Guevara had no time for theory in conversation, except as it applied to bringing the people to the revolution. But that was not a theoretical matter, it was a practical one; at least the part of it that was important was practical. While Guevara talked, he drew three-dimensional boxes on the back of an envelope. He drew lids for all sides, so his boxes were open-ended, endless, one leading off another. Guevara spoke very slowly, and said he was negotiating for one of the radios, but the difficulty was transportation. It always was: how to get from here to there. How to move, move quickly and with economy.

They did not talk long, and the conversation was often interrupted by Guevara's Cuban lieutenant, who kept reminding him of other appointments. But they parted friends, the colonel and Ché Guevara, promising to meet again when conditions permitted. Guevara was careful to say nothing of his destination.

The armed fist of the revolutionary front. Perhaps that is the way it would become, and one day he would awake and there would be forty Indians in his camp, all of them bringing food, bringing intelligence, all wanting guns, all of them prepared to accept the discipline.

—We have come to join, comrade.

—Where is your family?

—We have said good-bye to our families.

—How long will you stay?

—Until the revolution is made.

Perhaps Debray and the others were right, and that was the way it would become. But it was not that way now. It was only keeping going, and now only with the help of the American. Christ, it was risky, hitting and running with no accomplishment, morale down because nothing had happened. There was no revolution, only twelve men. That condition was more risky than bringing the American into it.

The colonel looked at Martinez, still against the wall, eyes burning, nasty. A nasty mood, the colonel thought. He would speak to Martinez again. Martinez didn't like any of it, liked least the thought of a gringo going on a mission, of the integrity of the guerrilla fractured by an outsider. North Americans were what Martinez liked least of all. Other foreigners came directly after, and their nationality did not matter to Martinez: Cubans, Argentinians, French, Chinese; they were all the same, plunderers of the soil, of the Indian soul. Martinez went along now for a while, and then he would challenge. The gringo could be killed after the mission, if Martinez insisted upon it. You couldn't have it all ways: to keep the guerrilla going, you had to have a success. The gringo was essential to the success. But of course Martinez was right about integrity.

—I will do it myself, *Jefe.*

—We can decide later.

—. . . with pleasure.

—We'll see.

—It's like having a bomb . . .

—Perhaps.

—I will do it myself.

—Perhaps.

—This man with the guerrilla is an offense.

—Yes, yes.

If they got through this, they would never need foreigners again, not the American Reardon or any of the others. Not Debray. The people would join the revolution when they became aware of it. Then it would be an irresistible force, like the wind on the land and the plain stretching to the mountains. The revolution would come to the land and the people who were there, and it had nothing to do with revolutions elsewhere.

But this gringo was strange. A few questions, no complaints, no difficulties. He neither agreed nor disagreed; he listened, made jokes, did not commit himself. Reardon understood where he was, but did not seem to care.

"Why only twelve?" Reardon took a cigarette from the colonel's package, lit it, and pushed the matches across the table. His head was clear now.

"It is a beginning."

"But very small."

"Correct."

"Where are they from?"

"Here and there. They are peasants, men of the fields."

"But good soldiers."

"Correct," the colonel lied.

"Tell me about the revolutionary conditions."

"It is a long story."

"We don't have time?" Reardon smiled.

"Señor, you look nervous."

"I am not nervous. I am tired and I have to take a piss."

"Take a piss, señor."

It is a very long story, but I will shorten it a little for you, Reardon. (The colonel spoke swiftly, the joking ended, Martinez gone now at a word). Please help yourself to the brandy. We have plenty of it.

You none of you understand what life is like here. You know all the familiar things, the climate, the disease, the illiteracy, the things that are done to a woman to kill her inside before she is thirty. At nine, they chew coca leaves and at twenty they are dull, their heads filled up with smoke. They do it to ease the pain of work in the fields, or of disease. They can clear the smoke with brandy, so they drink brandy. On the high plain, there is no fuel, so the Indians burn dung. The smoke collects at the top of the hut, and it is as a smokehouse. The smoke from shit keeps them warm. No other fuel is so cheap, or so available. Food? Wheat, barley, bread, and potatoes; twice a day.

They take the animals to market, to Acopara or to any of the other market towns, and because there was a sale somewhere else, because someone in the capital or in Buenos Aires or Chicago pushed a button, the price is down a few cents. The man returns to his hut with half the money he thought he would have. So that winter the family eats seed potatoes instead of planting them. The next summer, because there is no crop, there is famine. It is a murderous cycle: no one hears of the famine on the plain because the government does not govern here. Dictatorship! Shit! It is no government at all, except in the *barrios,* and I do not care for the *barrios;* that is, for the social planners and the builders. Let them take care of what goes on there. We are a separate problem, more complicated; much more complicated, señor. I am trying now to give you a sense of the objective conditions.

Most of the Indians own their own land, and in some places they share it with neighbors and in other places not. Close to the towns the land is owned by men who live elsewhere; all the best land is owned in that fashion. These landlords appoint local officials, who of course are obedient. But the government does not govern; in a small way, it occupies. But its effect is minor. The Indians exist apart from the government, and apart from the landlords. They have the wind instead. You do not find mention of the wind in your economic reports. Or the hail. Or the lightning. On this plain, the Indians believe the lightning is the hand of God. It strikes them indiscriminately, wherever they are, and it need not strike them directly to damage them. If it strikes in the vicinity of a child, it means that child has been touched, and will fall ill. You have seen the storms that come from the north, the lightning preceding them. Perhaps it has something to do with the altitude, twelve thousand feet on this plain, higher to the north and west, that there is lightning and so much of it. The wind gives him wind sickness, which competes with fright; both are usually cured with toads. Fright. Either way, there is nothing for the Indian to do but wait it out. He waits out the lightning and the wind, which kills his animals, and if it is strong enough, blows the huts away. Then if he survives that, the cold kills the animals and the children. You know that if an animal falls sick it is left to die; the Indian believes that nothing can save animals once they are sick. The animals are left to die, and often the children are left to die also.

Of course the Indians have devised a means of dealing with it. He is called the *paco,* a guide and a comfort, fifteen cents an exorcism. Thank God there are *pacos.* If there were none, we would have to invent them. I do not know what is more important to my Indians: *pacos,* children, or animals. Children, I think. But without the animals, no one would survive. Just as they would not survive without good spirits and bad, and the means to summon them or cast them out; in other words, without the *pacos.* Have you watched the Indians when the *pacos* come to drive the spirits away, and heal the sick? It would break your heart to look at them. They are praying to God.

Certain things are done, because conditions here are known. A model farm with a windmill is built. But the Indians, for reasons of their own, believe that windmills are manifestations of evil. And by coincidence, that year there is a drought. Why couldn't the drought wait for another year? The Indians believe it is the fault of the windmill and the model farm, so they demand its removal; the model farm and its improvements are forgotten. The Argentines send a hundred head of cattle to the high plain. They are especially sturdy stock, and if they survive will revolutionize the economy of the plain: a great step forward, the planners say, and at first a few Indians are enthusiastic. They are reserved but enthusiastic, and willing at least to wait and see. But in six months all the cattle are dead, victims of the altitude and the other conditions we have been speaking about. So the Indians shrug and continue. Next an economic team from the United Nations spends six weeks on the plain, and reports that only a few improvements are needed to make the land habitable, to support a civilization. They have a list of twenty items which includes electricity, a highway, a school, a post office, an infirmary, and a hydroelectric plant. They concede that this will cost money, which no one has and if they did would not spend here, so they propose the elimination of the only thing the people have, the six fiestas a year. It will be a saving of—what?—seven hundred dollars a year, which no doubt will be applied to the other things: a seven-hundred-dollar highway or a seven-hundred-dollar hydroelectric plant. Certainly. Of course.

Some of the North American planners have a solution of a different sort. It is to move all the Indians to the jungle. It is a permanent disaster area here, all the economists agree that the high plain will not support life, or a civilization. The jungle is fertile and underpopulated. It is warm. Crops will grow. There is no wind or lightning; no gales, no cold. A man can grow what he needs on a plot a tenth the size of what is required here. So send the Indians to the jungle, where they will be better off, where they can live, raise their families, and . . . progress. But the height here—ah, the height, the altitude, has expanded the lungs and re-arranged some of the other chemistry of the body. Into the lungs has come tuberculosis, although that is a disease almost unknown now among North Americans and Europeans. The Indians go into the jungle and find they have tuberculosis. They did not know it before. There are other viruses, diseases that flourish there in the jungle; the peasant has no immunity to them—except, of course, to stay where he is, on the plain. Naturally, there are no doctors or medicines below. The heat shocks the Indians, as the cold and the wind here shocks you. The plants and the animals bewilder him; the terrain makes him uneasy. He is frightened, a fish out of water. *The peasant has no immunity,* no defense against the jungle. He absorbs all of it, and then he dies. The young die along with the old, but mostly it is the old. No immunity, señor, except for the Indians to stay where they are. So in these conditions, the plain gives as well as takes.

Does it come a little clearer now?

The Indians understand only themselves, señor, their own people. They live in a world controlled by ghosts, by forces outside themselves. Whoever it is who controls the wind and the lightning is no more comprehensible than the tourist who throws coins out of the window of a railroad car (or does not). They live in a world they do not understand, among things they do not understand and see no reason for. Finally (it is the ultimate disgust), they learn of life in the *barrios.* Someone tells them; and having heard stories, they migrate to the coast, earn a few coins, live in encampments, without family or friends. They are used by the factories until they are sick, and then they come back to the high plain. In time most of the Indians come back to the plain and die.

Let me tell you a story, not very pleasant, but revealing. It is the story of the *pishtacos*. They are a small cannibal tribe that lives very far from here, high into the mountains. They are very remote and little is known about them, even among us who live here and have contact with them. They are a mysterious group, wanderers, and to the Indians they are devils. They kill their victims to extract the grease from their bodies. To some of the Indians, the *pishtacos* represent the purest form of evil.

Some years ago, some of your scientists came to a small village fifty miles west of here, a poor village near the border. It was an isolated place, with very little commerce and no connection with the outside. They came to study the ways of the inhabitants of the village, which (I repeat) were very primitive and interesting to the North American scientists. They came from a university with the blessing of the governor of the province; the mayor of the town welcomed them. They were to stay two weeks, asking questions concerning the lives of the people. The scientists were very tactful, and they all spoke the dialect of the region; they did not push themselves on the people, and by all accounts were careful to be polite and calm and not disruptive. But a day after they arrived, an old man disappeared from the village, vanished with no trace. He was a demented old man, and had often disappeared before to wander for days in the plain and then return. No notice was taken that day, or the day after; nothing was said until the people had time to think about it, to reach their own conclusions. The people, in their minds, connected the two events: the arrival of the North American scientists and the disappearance of the old man. Or to be precise: the old man's family was the first to make the connection. The rumors commenced immediately, and the people decided the scientists were *pishtacos,* come secretly to the village to abduct certain people and carry them away into the mountains. There had been an incident with them thirty years before, and what happened then became part of the myths of the village, part of its life; parents would frighten their children with the story, but everyone believed it. This time not everyone accepted it at first, but soon the evidence was overwhelming. The visitors were so different in appearance, so peculiar in the way they spoke and ate their food, and in the way they behaved; the questions they asked; the machines they carried. It became clear to the people that the purpose of the visitors was malevolent. Questions which were at first innocent became sinister. To the people of the village, the scientists were menacing visitors. History was repeating itself.

Of course in the beginning the North Americans suspected nothing, and went on with their work with tape recorders and pads and pencils. The people were not helpful in answering questions, but that is often the case with these . . . expeditions. But on the fourth day of their visit, the people surrounded the house where they were staying. At first it was harrassment. A few stones were thrown and there were angry words. In the center of the mob was the family of the old man, now entirely convinced that the scientists were *pishtacos,* and their kinsman the first victim. On the fifth day, the people laid seige to the house with heavy clubs. There was no way for the North Americans to get word to the outside. The mayor was helpless, and I am not certain he did not sympathize with the mood of the town; rumors continued to grow, fed each day by the old man's failure to reappear, and reached a peak when the *pacos* of the town—men who had remained in their houses, indifferent and taking no part—joined the people.

So there was this: the next day, after a morning of shouting and threats and beating on the walls of the house, the people broke in and murdered the scientists. They murdered them like this. They strung them up on the rafters, a heavy cord under the arms, bound one to the other and to the ceiling beams, so that they hung down like sides of beef. Each inhabitant of the village had a turn with the club and flailed it until he was exhausted. The North Americans cried out, pleaded their innocence, offered money, offered to leave, anything—but the villagers, a mob now, were not listening. One can imagine the terror of the gringos, confronted with . . . history, señor, and no way to escape it. The scientists could not answer the only question that could have saved them: where the old man was, and why he had gone off. At the end of the day, the villagers fired the building with the scientists inside. They stood around it in a circle, the entire village, watching it burn. The people took the remains of the North Americans to the plain, where they carefully wrapped the ashes in sacks and buried them.

The next day, everything was normal in the town. I am sure you are familiar with the attitude; it is not peculiar to Indians. Where everyone is guilty, no one is guilty. And besides, we are not talking of guilt but of exorcism. The people went back to their business. A week after that, the old man, crazy from the wind and the lightning at night, returned. Oh, they said, the old man is back. The old one has returned at last. They connected the reappearance of the old man with the death of the North Americans, the *pishtacos* who arranged for his abduction in the first place. The death of the North Americans made possible the return of the old man. It was an unexpected and miraculous favor, and fascinated the villagers; nothing quite like it had ever happened before. You see, there is a certain fatalism: when a thing is done, it is done and nothing can undo it. It is a part of the past, as a stone worn away on a mountain slope, falling and disturbing other stones, changing the conditions; and impossible to put it all back the way it was, impossible to . . . restore the original. A stone changes position, and changes thereby the shape of the earth forever. The death of the scientists proved the perception of the people: if the scientists had been innocent, they would not have died and the old man would have not returned. Does lightning strike only the innocent? The event was part of the past, and therefore contributed to the present; to undo it was to undo history, to change the shape of the earth, and to meditate on it a pointless and unrevealing act. The Indian does not change history, he accommodates himself to it. Since he does not seek to change that which controls him, he does not take responsibility for . . . events.

What do we make of that? To the villagers then, there was not the slightest doubt that their visitors were devils—and more than that, had come to represent civilization. They were the forces of control, the malevolence that operates the wind and the lightning, and the conditions of life on this plain, the desperation, the death, all the unknowns that govern the lives of the Indians. The people had reconciled themselves to these conditions—until the threat, the menace, became too great to bear. Until it became intolerable. The people protect themselves with the means available to them.

We are fighting the *pishtacos,* those who kill the living, squeezing the grease from the bodies of the people; the forces of control. You too, Reardon. Perhaps you worst of all. The civilized devil. Bring an Indian to God, and forget for a moment the manner in which he must live, and the forces with which he must contend. Or bring an Indian to the irrigation, and never mind the state of his soul. I have it both ways, señor, because the only answer is one which neither the church nor the government can accept. It is to give the plain, all of it, back to the Indians to do with it what they please. And the rest of you get out. No church, no government; no scientists or economists, no padres. You are playing toy soldiers here, señor; the holy cards and the money you spend are for you, not for us. None of it matters to us; it matters to you. What are you doing on this plain? What is it that brings you here? Why are you here, Reardon?

Chapter Five

THERE WERE TWO weathered stone buildings, set high on a hill in a wood outside a mill town in southern Ohio. The town was in a valley and could not be seen from the fields. The hills rolled off in green and brown, and at dusk the green turned into black when the light failed. On hot summer days the smoke from the mills settled into the valley, and spread a gray haze, as if from morning mist. In winter, soot covered the snow. The men worked the land and meditated in silence, thoughts at one with the fields, the men moving like sleepwalkers, tight worlds reaching to the universe. Outside, life pressed in through the haze, came in the sounds of the road that passed the iron gate.

It had been the mansion of an industrialist, built in the style of an English country house with walnut walls and heavy iron chandeliers. The industrialist gave it to the Order when he moved south, away from the cold and the haze, and it became a hermitage whose windows were filled with leaded glass. When Reardon marched the corridors, he heard not his own feet slapping the stones, but the feet of others, earlier solitaries. Obsessed by sounds: the onionskin pages of the Bible, the rustle of cloth, the clink of spoons in metal tureens, the splash of water. Obsessed by smells: candlewax and wine, the grittiness of old stones, the brocade of a surplice, a delicious wood fire. Sights: the mist that came at evening, the drape of the hood of the monk leading the procession, the swing of the thurible, the tilt of the corridors, the picture of Jesus torn from a magazine and pasted on the walls of his cell. High in the tower at night, he saw red beacons from the town winking at each other. One winked three times to the other's twice, and that was the erratic rhythm of the world from a mill town in Ohio. BlinkaBLINKbliBLINKnkaBLINK. And Reardon watching it, chin cupped in his hands like a gargoyle at Notre Dame, pointing his tongue at the lights.

The hours alone inside his head became unendurable, the noise of silence permanent, and his withdrawal was never complete. Four years of signals, one monk to another, of signals at prayer and at work, signals while pacing the measured steps to the garden, signals like small boys at study hall. From the beginning he learned to keep his eyes low, and the signals and silence were a comfort. After a year he was worried, and much later in despair. *No contact, Father; no contact.* And then after four years, a trip into town, an eye-averting embarrassed journey through squalor and noise to the railroad station to meet a visitor, and then to the town's church for prayer. Reardon fell to his knees gratefully, desperate to retreat from the sounds and the sights of what he knew then, understood absolutely, to be reality: the lonely look of the railroad station at afternoon, the oily wood and the iron cage of the stationmaster, and behind the building, in an alley, a derelict, down and out, the wine bottle smashed in pieces beside him, a small boy looking at the filthy clothes and the dirty stubble and the battered face, grinning. People made way for Reardon, observed him cautiously from the corners of their eyes. He was disconnected, outside of himself, and returned to the car alone to await the train. At the church, nuns served him juice and tried to talk; but he could not look them in the face, or speak, and leaned against the church walls for support. He drank with his eyes on the floor, and left for prayer immediately. But in the car on the way back to the monastery, Reardon could not keep his eyes from the shacks along the road, and the people standing in front of him staring vacantly at the passage of vehicles—cars, trucks, buses; the people on the front porch staring into the middle distance, hands tucked into the back pockets of overalls, swaying like saplings, and the movement of children on front stoops. The telephone poles snapped by and Reardon took in all the details and then, shaken, returned to the safety of the interior of the sedan, fastened on the center strip of the highway, while praying for swift passage to his cell.

News from the outside came in code, and it was always murderous news. It spread in a twinkling and the building was quickly lost in prayer, praying for the soul of a Pope or a President. On certain feast days, he was thurifer, and he would remember for the rest of his life the clink of the chains that held the censer, the shuffle of feet, the breathing that came with prayer, the dark robes and hoods hiding faces, and the aroma of incense behind him, trailing like a spectre. Then to the cell and on one's own knees, trembling, the collapse into bed, marking off time in ten-minute intervals, one thousandandone one thousandandtwo, listening to the breathing of the others thinking, awake in thought. After two years he could not know whether he was awake or asleep; uncertain, he dragged a fingernail across the stone beside the pallet, listening to the scrape, feeling the stone. Hands locked behind his head, he lay on the pallet, moving slightly, shifting from side to side, listening to the noise the movement made on the straw, the strands touching and rubbing, caressing. Visions came to mind, and dispersed; tight, he struggled to conjure them, bring them back; but they fled, gone as quickly as they had come, and gone forever. Skin drawn across his face tight as a death's head, the sound of prayer thundered in his ears. He recollected the blinkaBLINK of the lights above the town, and it mingled with the other; he could not get them straight, and could not see them from the window of his cell. And all this time, the sounds of the others: some snores, murmurings, some turnings, a Chinese who talked in his sleep. There were footfalls somewhere, someone walking to someplace. A monk was up to take a leak, and Reardon lay in his bed, listening to the breathing, trying to breath silently as though dead, listening to the water. A door opened in the corridor and there were footfalls again. Finally all the sounds were one, and after that he slept.

The world stayed outside, at arm's length, away from the devotions of the monastery. Reardon read the lessons and watched the lights, and in his fourth year journeyed to the railroad station and the church in town. But that was all. The letters came, eight each year, and they spoke of his sacrifice, his iron discipline, in working for God and the church, for humanity in his own way; God bless you, the letters ended, God bless. They assumed his life was hard, bad food, no heat, a life of longing and mortification, of deprivation. So he could not tell them that there was no mortification, that there was nothing. Periods of consultation followed periods of prayer and study and evaluation, and although his confessor was doubtful and urged him into more prayer, Reardon knew he was not capable of final retreat, was neither a solitary nor a contemplative; finally he doubted the *use* of it all. To his mind came one of Merton's worries. *What is the good of a priest who does not trust God, and who has no practical belief in His power...* Was it trust? When he tried to understand the monastery and the world, how and where they connected and how and why he had entered the one and remained in it, then everything else became a question. It came apart. Reardon renounced his order—*no trust, Father; no trust,*—resigned, and returned to the world. But he told them only a fraction of what he knew.

The colonel had fallen silent, weary from the exertion, and opened another bottle of brandy. The wind was outside and the rain, too, drumming at the door and the windows. The wet came into the house along with the wind. Reardon had been given a poncho, and he had that wrapped tightly around him; but it was cold. The colonel reached into a sack and pulled out two cans of sardines. Very carefully and slowly, with cramped cold fingers, he pried the tops off, and handed one can to Reardon and kept one for himself. They had talked most of the night, and now ate in silence. Reardon ate deliberately, with no great appetite, feeling the oil on his fingers and on his chin, washing the fish down with the harsh brandy. The colonel excused himself, wiping his hands on his trousers, and disappeared into the darkness at the rear of the room.

Reardon concentrated on the fish, thinking of all he had read of the Indians and life on the high plain; what he had read and heard of the rebels in the mountains. Between the appearance and the reality falls the shadow; some shadow. He examined the map behind the desk. There was no pattern to the arrangement of the pins, which he supposed represented encounters of one sort of another. They were widely scattered, some near villages, some in the mountains, engagements at random. Reardon did not recognize the terrain, but surmised they were very near the border if not over it. No, not over it, the colonel had said; but very near. The camp was not indicated on the map.

When the colonel returned, he carried with him a large notebook wrapped in oilcloth. He removed the oilcloth and dropped the book on the table in front of Reardon. "Read it," he said, tapping the table. "It will tell you about us, better than I can, more accurately; drink some brandy while you read it."

Reardon drew the kerosene lamp closer to him, and picked up the book and began to read at random. It was a diary of the guerrilla, a pavan of disaster, of storm and illness and misstep and stupidity; an occasional success, and not much to be made of the success. Reardon read:

> 21 July. We walked until early morning, drowsing during the last hour and feeling quite cold. The winds have caught up with us now, and don't let us go. We are ill with edema; food is low, and the ammunition shipments have not arrived. No indication when they will come, if they do come. There are complaints . . .
>
> 25 July. A dispute arose between Mono and Juanito, and I had to settle it, without being sure I settled it justly. We are all feeling better now, with a cow slaughtered and fresh vegetables. We split the guerrilla at daybreak, and by afternoon there was still no sign of the others. It is not an area any of us know well. I kept Mono with me and sent Juanito with the others. There is very bad blood

now . . . Finally we came together at nightfall. There is a prospect for tomorrow if the rain ceases.

26 July. The errors began early in the morning. After we withdrew from the camp, Hernan and Tomas set out to explore a place to set an ambush, pushing more deeply into the valley and eventually separating themselves from the rest of us. It took three hours to reconnect, and the day was lost thrashing about in hostile country. No soldiers came. We missed the marked trail, and so were lost most of the rest of the day. What we need is a navigator . . .

1 August. Back at the camp, and conferences with Juanito and Mono and the others. That situation seems better, and now we try to make a strategy. All have their say, even the youngster, but we fell to talking of tactics and the need for discipline. Juanito and Mono want to make a quick strike now, and forget about supplies and preparation; it dominates their thoughts, and I concede they have a point, although my instincts are all against it.

5 August. After a day of continuous climbing, we came to a river with good water running due east. We are better now with food, and plenty of ammunition. Mono located the cache, which was exactly where we were told it would be. There was a Browning and three Stens and one hundred rounds of ammunition; it is a help, particularly the Browning, but I wish the other weapons would arrive. The communications are impossible, and we must improve them. Time, time wasted and thrown away, and there is not much time, especially for us. But late in the day we found a pig, and after a hectic chase we caught it and ate it. A feast for everyone, and the bath in the river was good, too.

20 August. The guerrilla: Juanito and Mono are accomplished and disciplined most of the time, and Francisco and Tomas will be all right after another few months. They are not used to the closeness and the construction of movement, and the care with which we must prepare our ground. The boy Hernan is a worry. But he is willing and very strong, and if he will listen he will be an asset. But he thinks it is a game, "the glorious victory of the revolution." He thinks the others are saints. They are coming along, although all of them miss their families. They are not accustomed to surviving themselves, with no help and no brandy or coca when they want it. But the certainty of victory keeps us all going, and what we need now is patience.

5 September. A patrol stumbled into us; we killing three and taking two prisoner. They are so frightened! The officer immediately threw down his pistol and gave himself up. He was weeping. The three who were killed put up a little fight, but not much. I rushed forward with the Browning when I heard the firing, but it was already under control. The first fight in a month! And the best! We set the prisoners free after lecturing to them, but I wonder if we shouldn't simply kill them. It is what Juanito wants. It would be a simple matter (a patrol would just disappear), but still I don't like it. The ambush was beautifully done, exactly as it ought to be; no one slipped the trap. Juanito says that now the two prisoners will have descriptions of us, our weapons and our method of operation. I argue that that is good, that rumors will spread. He disagrees. He took their shoes and their uniforms, and after they buried their dead we left them to make it back in their undershorts. The weapons of three of them were damaged in the firing, but still we captured a Sten and the officer's sidearm (which does not seem to fire properly). The guerrilla took no casualties . . . our spirits are as high as the mountains.

10 September. We must keep discipline, for again today there was a needless injury. Mono broke from the ambush and was wounded in the leg. It slowed us up, first because of the surgery and then because of the difficulty of moving along the trail with Mono in the sling. Juanito dug the bullet out in a very professional way; he and Mono seemed to have made it up. No casualties on the other side. I think there were only two of them anyway, and from Urbano's position and the angle of the bullet I think he was hit by one of us. The others, Juanito in particular, complain again of the strategy. They want a major strike against an installation. They want something that will tell the others that we are here, and serve notice on the army, too; but the others know, and the

army needs no notices from us. Juanito says that the morale of
the guerrilla is slack, not as high as it should be; I tell him I know
it. But we do not have the arms for the sort of attack he wants. A
major attack would finish us if the slightest thing went wrong.
There is the Browning, and that is all; and it is not enough. Still,
Juanito has a point. The arms shipment is expected any time, and
it cannot come soon enough. Now we are over the border and we
went hungry again today.

20 September. Francisco left us to reconnoiter a house in the valley, and we have not seen him. He may have deserted, although it
is possible he lost his way, possible too that he was seized by a patrol, though unlikely. He has kept to himself this past week, eating
little and looking at me with a dark face. He was a good man.
Mono's leg is now healing with no complications, but still he cannot walk. The others complain, now of the food, now of the tactics. At least we have the camp, where we are completely safe. Of
course we must abandon it within the next few months; too risky.
We take too many chances as it is, and now I must exert authority
again and again to keep us afloat. Discipline! Discipline! Discipline! That is all there is to this thing, a long wait until the moment is right and the mood changes; a long struggle until one day
you are not a dozen but two thousand. It is exactly as Fidel said of
Ché, "He considered himself a soldier of this revolution without
even worrying about surviving it." They worry about survival
here. They worry about death and their families, and where their
wives are and what is happening now with the crops and the animals, whether the children are well. It is a war of small bites. We
bite them with three dead here, two wounded there. And we lose
a good man a month. We lost a good man last month. We lost An-
tonio, and now perhaps we have lost Francisco. I feel it: we have.
And we can't afford it. We can afford it less than they can afford a
battalion dead. The peasants are not coming to us. It is a vicious
circle: they will not come to us until we are successful, and we
will not be successful until they come to us . . . With Francisco
gone, we must now definitely give up the camp.

11 October. Political education in Lito today. About twenty people listened to me, and then to Juanito. We asked them to help us and they said they would, but no one volunteered. The people seem to agree when we told them about the government, about what was happening in the capital, the corruption on the land and with animal prices, and then we told them the land was theirs, belonged to them, all of it; the cities, too, Juanito said, the cities were theirs. One old man was puzzled. He shook his head when Juanito mentioned the cities, and I asked him why. He shrugged and said, "I don't like cities, so you can give them to the others here." Juanito did not know what to say to that (neither did I). They believe what we tell them, but will do nothing about it. They do not understand us, what we are doing and why we are doing it. They want to ask us why, but they do not; they sit and listen quietly and agree. We paid them for some food, and they seemed grateful for that. Juanito bluntly told them that it was their duty to support us, since we were fighting for them, etc., but they turned away from him. They said their lives were difficult. They wished us success. We went the way we came . . .

Reardon put the diary down, and slid it across the table.

"It is not the Sierra Maestra, is it?"

"We are not the Cubans, señor. I am not Castro. This man who led you here, Martinez. Martinez is not Ché."

"Surely there are others . . ."

The colonel smiled. "What others? Where are they?" He put the notebook back into the oilcloth pouch. "We do what we can, an ambush here, a sabotage there. Nothing of importance yet. When we come into town for the night, we listen to the radio. In Asia, the forces of liberation are winning and winning against the entire American army. Castro has consolidated in Cuba, and others are successfully at work in Peru, Bolivia. Take Cuba, señor.

How did he do it? What were the details? I would like to know the factual sequence of events, events stripped of theory; no poetry, Reardon, just how it happened. When did the peasants come to him? What made them? How did he keep his weapons working? Where did the money come from? How did he use his communications? How did he *control*? He began in the middle of the nineteen fifties with one dozen men . . . "

"He had Batista," Reardon said.

"Batista was worth a regiment," the colonel agreed, smiling and pouring two fresh brandies. "Well, we listen to the radio, and Juanito and the others do not understand why it goes so slowly. I understand it better than they. The colonialism has been subtle . . . it is not fertile soil for revolution, this high plain; I know that . . . the others do not. Juanito doesn't. We have no Batistas here." He paused, fingers drumming on the table. Reardon did not reply.

"I come from across the border," the colonel said.

"You are not from the plain?"

"There is plenty of plain, señor, and I come from the part across the border. The plain is the same either place. Perhaps it is a bit colder where I come from; the people, perhaps, are not quite so poor. But it is not much of a distinction." He paused again. "I had three years in a high school, when I was in the army. It was an army school, but there was a library. There, and in the town too. Good libraries, Reardon."

"I know."

"Then I lived in the capital—this one, not the other. I joined the army here." He picked up the notebook, and pointed it at Reardon. "You don't hear anything about this guerrilla because there is nothing to hear yet, nothing of importance. What happens, they are able to keep quiet."

"But the rumors . . . " Reardon began.

He brushed it aside, sweeping his hand across the desk. "Yes, of course, *hombre*. Because we hurt them so little. There is no need to make publicity, except to the Americans. But they cannot stop rumors, and this is wonderful country for rumors. Rumors are worth a regiment. But the rumors are for others, not for us. I can get drunk on things other than rumors. Our great victory, the victory of five September, three killed, two captured, the lieutenant so scared he wet his pants. What do we make of that? What do I tell the people who send the supplies, the ones who give us the money and the arms? Ah, comrades—the enemy is in flight, the capital at seige; a glorious victory, the victory of five September, three imperialist lackeys killed, two others stripped and sent back to the garrison in their underpants! Don't comfort me with that, or ask me to comfort others. Any guerrilla can fix an ambush. I can fix an ambush with the ease you light a cigarette. An ambush is very, very easy and very, very safe. You can do it with six men, two up front with clear fields of fire, one on each side of the trail, the others in the rear. It takes a little preparation. You put a distraction somewhere, a dead goat, a dead bird, anything. You get your two front men in place. Then you take the other four men and place them in a fan. The first two let the patrol pass, then they hit, and drop flat so as not to be shot themselves by bullets from the four ahead. The patrol is in a complete trap, the four in a fan cut down the others. It is like shooting ducks on a pond, señor. Very simple, so long as each man does his job, does what he is told *precisely.*"

Reardon was silent.

"We criticize. Criticize! Criticize! Criticize! When there are no big things to criticize, criticize the small ones. Never, never become satisfied. Write the criticisms down. Repeat them singly and together. Something is always being done wrong, imperfectly. To survive in a guerrilla, a man must be a perfectionist. The discipline must be complete."

Reardon said: "Martinez?"

"Martinez is impatient, yes. But he understands the discipline, understands the need for it, and will accept it. Martinez . . . "

The two met in the army, Martinez conscripted in the capital and posted to a regiment stationed near the border. It was there he met Pacheco, then a captain, who had already gathered half a dozen men for the nucleus of a guerrilla. Martinez left a mother and five sisters behind on the plain, to find work in the capital. He bought himself a laborer's job in a *yanqui* tire factory and worked at it for two years, saving money and living with two families in an outlying district. He had saved three hundred dollars and planned to take it and return to the plain, buy land, and become a farmer. But one afternoon when he was walking home from work, the civil guard arrested him for theft; a week later, he was in the army.

The colonel said that Martinez wanted to marry, but had not. In the meantime, there were girls in the pueblos. He decided not to have any family until the plain was taken from those who controlled it. He and the colonel agreed on that point, and spoke of it often. He put his life into the guerrilla, and now the one was the same as the other. He said it would be very difficult to give up, when the time came to give it up.

"He was taught politics in the capital, señor," the colonel said. At night, a worker in the plant organized meetings and brought books and pamphlets to read. They discussed the revolution elsewhere, drew lessons from it and applied the lessons to conditions on the high plain. At the age of twenty, Martinez taught himself to read Spanish from the books and pamphlets, and now he was quite certain what he wanted for himself and for the plain. The thing that had to come before anything else was the expulsion of the gringos. Nothing else was so important, so crucial to progress; everything, but that was complicated.

"So he is impatient, señor. Sometimes he has difficulty seeing the need for discipline . . . "

"Yeah," Reardon said.

"The others are not so clear about it as Martinez."

"Right."

"And you, Reardon. Do you concentrate on discipline?"

"Ah, no," Reardon said.

"No? Odd."

"No, we concentrate on praise. Optimism. No problem so difficult it cannot be solved; no situation so desperate it cannot be saved. It was the foundation of the country until recently, Colonel."

"Explain, please."

"Well, didn't we lose a war? And stand in danger of losing other wars? It is very difficult so we end up in places like Acopara. Why not here? It is the last frontier, and that is why we are here, some of us. The frontier is congenial, less restricting, less complicated. We deal with the new rather than the old. It is the old that puzzles us." Reardon paused for a moment, then added, "or perhaps the other way around."

"Why did you lose the war?" He was leaning forward on the desk, interested.

"That war doesn't bear on this one," Reardon said.

"Perhaps not. But . . . "

"We are not into this war yet."

"No."

"You should wish we were. If Batista was worth a regiment, the Americans should be worth a division. Maybe two divisions."

The colonel was looking at him blankly. "I do not understand."

"Neither do I, Colonel." He was weary. His mouth was dry and dirty from the cigarettes, and his stomach sour from brandy. "I am not aware of the United States. I lived there in a place called Boise."

"That is in the United States?"

"Yes and no."

Reardon got up and stretched, and walked over to the fire. The wood had burned, and now there were only hot coals. He stared into the red, momentarily hypnotized by the glow. His back ached and he rubbed it. When the hell would there be sleep? But the colonel showed no signs of fatigue.

"What is the difference between the two countries, this one and the other one?" Reardon asked.

"As I told you, no difference. The one is perhaps a bit poorer and colder."

"Well, if you had a choice—which would you rather live in?"

"There is no difference, señor. The one is the same as the other. It is the same plain, so the countries involved are not important."

"Would you feel differently if you were born mestizo?"

The colonel grunted. He was bored with speculation.

"How would I know that? I was not born mestizo. It is a ridiculous question. What point is there to answer it?"

"I'm curious."

He shrugged. "It can't be answered."

"If you were born mestizo, with a little money and a formal education. Say, you were a doctor. If you had a good farm or a good business . . ."

"Yes, all right. I suppose ... if I was one of those bastards, differently, sure."

"How?"

"How could I possibly know how?"

"You have fallen away from the church?"

He nodded.

"Well, you would not have fallen away from the church if you were mestizo."

"Yes, fine. So what? Look, Reardon ..." He muttered something in dialect. "Look, let us get back to the radio station, the business at hand."

"Birds at swim, Colonel."

"Look. You have fallen away from the church? Yes. But would you have fallen away from the church if you were Rockefeller?"

"No," Reardon said. "Of course not. Certainly not. Why?"

The colonel looked at him, irritated and perplexed. He pointed to the map. "The radio station, Reardon."

"One more thing, you have the guerrilla."

"Correct."

"Well, there you are."

"Shit," the colonel said.

He was looking at Reardon with large, innocent eyes, feeling the stubble on his chin and frowning. And Reardon was looking at him and thinking: right. Right, the bastard is very nearly crazy. Crazy with something. A guerrilla in this country was insanity. Or it was suicidal. Nits. A guerrilla of nits, ticks, and small bites. Seizing the radio station, holding it for fifteen minutes, was minor vandalism. None of the Indians would give a damn, and a lot of men would be killed to no purpose. And if it failed, it would be the end of the rebellion because the colonel and his twelve men *were* the rebellion; it existed wherever the guerrilla was, and nowhere else. Now it was at the camp. In a week it would be someplace else. But *El Jefe*, Colonel Pacheco, would have his victory and his headline, REBELS SEIZE RADIO STATION AT ACOPARA. Those broadcasts from across the border that spoke of Castro and the North Vietnamese army would now speak of the new army, a new rebel army in another place, strong enough and confident enough to raid a town; radio station at Acopara . . . *seized*. It was inspiriting. But the colonel was a canny man, savvy as they say, and he had a method; his men backed him, not without complaint, but still they backed him. He had a method and an analysis, and he was as stubborn as the people he was trying to win. The soil grew both kinds. Reardon recalled a friend at the monastery, who for a year pursued Teilhard de Chardin through the *noosphere*. It was a pursuit as single-minded as any in the history of the monastery; if someone had written a company history, this monk would rate a long footnote. He went at it like a man working a million-piece jigsaw puzzle of the galaxy. For all Reardon knew, he was still at it, hunched over the table, a piece of blue sky in his hand, turning and fitting it this way and that, convinced that if it fit, *if the one piece fit,* it would lead to all the other pieces; the riddle of the universe would be solved, there for everyone to see, complete, fastened together, the universe as chain mail, Teilhard the creator.

But the colonel: twelve men and his ambition. Mostly it was method and analysis, and that was sometimes all you needed. That, and a framework and guns. And confidence. Others had begun with not much more, often less. Sometimes the single-minded spirit triumphed. It had happened before. The government was not solid, God knows; it had nothing but guns and the fact that it was there, in place. It existed side by side with the army and the church, which insisted that it prevail. They squatted side by side by side, pendulum clocks that wound each other.

Reardon was walking slowly to the window, feeling the fatigue in his legs and his head. He pulled the black curtain to one side and looked out. "Why me, Colonel?" he asked finally, his face to the glass, his forehead resting gently on the cold. "Of all those who know the radio, why me?"

"Why not? The choice was limited. Three or four men only, and it had to be an American."

"An American," Reardon repeated.

"A man with detachment, available," the colonel added.

"By all means."

"Your sympathies are well known."

Reardon looked at him from the window. They were not well known at all. He was an invisible man to the people of Acopara, a friend and confidant of gas-station attendants and mestizo waiters, merchant-doctors and an Indian lady who sold alpaca sweaters at the railroad station. Of course there were the officials who invited him twice a year to national day ceremonies, fiestas. Those were days with excellent opportunities to demonstrate solidarity with the people. "I would like to know your informants," Reardon said.

The colonel shrugged, and moved back in his chair. He half-smiled and lit a cigarette, looking at Reardon standing by the window, his face to the glass. "We were told you did not care for this government. It was nothing you said; it was an attitude, the inquiries you made. Not every one in this guerrilla believed it. But I believed it. It is not a matter of great importance to me. Don't push too hard, señor."

The older man continued to talk, Reardon watching him. It did not make sense. But there was something appealing in what the colonel was saying. It was crap, and Reardon didn't believe it, and he wasn't sure whether the colonel believed it. Maybe he was just talking.

"You got me because there was no one else."

The colonel stopped.

"There wasn't anybody else. No Indian would do it, and no American, either. I was the easiest American, correct, Colonel?"

"Perhaps true."

"All true," Reardon said. "The people don't believe in this revolution. Most of them don't know about it, and those who do don't want it. Twelve men, Colonel, and a plain the size of—what?— Utah, Arizona, Ecuador? There are three Indians who know almost as much about that radio as I do, and each of them more than enough for your requirements. Why not them?"

"Difficulties," he said.

"Damn right. Difficulties. No one wanted to risk his neck, or risk capture by the army. Or getting killed. You have got twelve men on this plain who are willing to risk themselves, and that is all you have got. The others are afraid."

The colonel nodded, not indicating agreement but merely that he had heard. Reardon took a cigarette from the package on the table. He lit it and watched the smoke curl to the ceiling, breaking from the draft of cold air as it rose. Pacheco watched him steadily, his face older now in the gloom of the hut, sagged in fatigue, the outlines blurred and run together, a picture out of focus. He was a middle-aged man and all the lines on his face showed, and cast shadows down his cheeks. His hands were cupped around the brandy glass, strong but rutted and pitted like an old road. He was playing now against very long odds. Others had done it, but the soil of other countries was more hospitable than this one. He let Reardon go on.

"What happens after the raid?"

"It is of no importance to me," the colonel said.

"So?"

"You go," the colonel said, expressionless.

"Where?"

"Anywhere you want. Back to your work, your holy cards. Back to your games."

"Sure. I just walk away from the radio."

"Why not?" the colonel asked, his voice soft. "We put the guerrilla in your hands, and now it is up to you, the padre of the revolution." He spoke very quietly, tapping the brandy glass on the table. He lowered his voice further, almost to a whisper, and spoke quickly: "You understand the importance of the radio, and the necessity for doing it now. Not in three months or six, but doing it now. And doing it properly, the way it must be done. Not an error. No false steps."

Reardon said he understood that, and sat back and watched the smoke go to the ceiling. He was not thinking, he was contemplating, bone-tired, so tired his movements seemed in slow-motion, and his thoughts stuck like a broken record. If someone had shaken him, he would have awakened as if from reverie. He watched the smoke. The colonel arose and went again to the rear of the hut. He returned carrying two shotguns, handed one to Reardon and motioned for him to follow. Dawn was breaking, cold and very gray, iron-gray with low clouds scudding across the ceiling of the sky. The rocks, flecked with green moss, were touched with the gray. Standing at the edge of the ridge, Reardon flipped his cigarette and watched it bounce, small red sparks flying. The two men left the camp and began the scramble down the escarpment to the valley floor. The colonel said they would eat black duck, *chauinquird,* for breakfast.

The rain had ended and the wind died with dawn, but the rocks were slippery with little puddles of water among them. The Indian and Reardon made their way carefully down the slope, holding the shotguns wide of their bodies, using the free hand to balance themselves on the rocks as they descended. At the bottom was a river, dammed with rocks and brush into a pond. Reardon already saw the ducks flying in formation, mostly in threes, small and very fast, black against the gray sky. They came over a small stony rise to the east, fluttered in, setting wings to hit the far end of the pond. A morning mist covered the valley floor and the water, a mist so fine and tranquil that Reardon began to smile and forget his fatigue, and smiled and enjoyed himself all the way down the slope to the rocks that lined the water.

There were no trees. There were the high rocks, big as houses, and the earth and the scrub and the water beyond. They watched the pattern of the flight for a moment, leaning their guns against the rocks, resting. Then the colonel leaned toward Reardon and whispered: *We will ambush. I will move to those rocks there*—he motioned to a place between two rocks where he could stand to fire—*and set up a block. You move to the edge of the pond, there*—the colonel pointed to a place fifty yards down, a natural blind among the rocks which he could reach without being seen—*and take them as they come in high. By rights you will miss a few and they will fly to me. Black duck, Reardon.*

Reardon, gripping the shotgun by the breech, nodded and took half a dozen shells from the colonel. They waited until the mist cleared. *Silence, señor,* the colonel said, putting two fingers to his mouth, then patting the air; *silence yourself,* Reardon said and crouched lower behind the rock. It was an unnecessary precaution: these birds would not spook, not in a hundred years. They flew bold as cavaliers, owning the sky and the water. The water was the color of slate, and flat. The land rolled away for miles, and then rose again, gray and heavy under the clouds. The mist slowly lifted, and the colonel touched Reardon's shoulder and moved off. *Luck,* he said. Reardon made his way down the slope, the fifty yards to the edge of the pond between two boulders where he could peek out and see the ducks flying, and in the water on the far side. More were coming in from the east. They were very long shots, and Reardon looked at the shells again. Hand-packed, they were the equivalent of two-shot, a goose load, fine for long range. The ducks would be tough, strong from beating against the wind and surviving at that height. The shotgun was a single-barreled, single-shot...fowling piece. No other word for it. Brand and maker were long since worn from the metal. Its pine stock was polished the color of coffee grounds, nicked and scarred, never oiled except by sweat and rain. The barrel was rusted to a grainy gray, clammy to the touch, its BB sight missing; an ungraceful shotgun, but so well used that Reardon handled it with great care. Using it was like sitting in a friend's favorite armchair.

The blacks began to move. They were coming from the east in pairs and threes, an occasional single, reconnoitering a little, looping high over the pond in tight beautiful arcs, then falling and skidding into the water like breaking skiers. Reardon watched them over the lip of the stone, wondering where to take the first one, worrying that there was no dog and thinking about dropping the bird in the middle and then having to wade out and get it. He looked to his right, but the colonel was out of sight. He must be ready now. Do it slow, very slowly and gently; choose the bird and the piece of sky. Fast-winged, a black now came over the water, swinging close to Reardon. As the bird turned, making the first brake with his wings, the man stood and followed him with the gun and fired; the man and the bird were one and the bird was hit, its marvelous rhythm gone all to pieces, the man still following and the bird, silent-falling, one wing splayed, dropped straight. Then chaos. There were twenty birds on the pond and, at the shot, all of them rose, the placid water now rippled and disturbed and the silence cut by cries. Reardon looked at the black in the water, tiny waves moving from its still body. It was a dead hit. Reardon heard one shot, and silence, and another shot, and knew that the colonel was taking them as they flew off the pond. Reardon was standing with the shotgun, the smell and taste of powder in his mouth, looking at the dead bird and remembering the fall, the break in flight, the jerk of the wings as the shot hurt him. Birds were everywhere now, flying from all directions. Reardon concentrated with difficulty, and raising the gun fired once and missed; shot again, missed again; shot a third time and hit. But his eyes kept returning to the first bird dead in the water, heavy now where the light hit the water in streaks, the color of mercury, the first bird floating into shore with the other. Reardon stared at it a long time, remembering the hunts in different places, in Idaho and Maryland on other mornings, four or five friends up well before dawn, and the prospect of a huge breakfast later after the shooting. But the birds there were suspicious, accustomed to gunners.

He absent-mindedly fished a cigarette from his shirt pocket and lit it and enjoyed the memories, which came in a rush without order or precedence; shooting with his friends, his father, being taught how to break and clean an over-and-under: *Goddam it, never point a gun at anybody, when you're cleaning it or any other time; the unloaded gun kills people,* the polished mahogany gun case in the library, the yellow and red Hoppe's patches box, his father's oversized waders and cartridge case, which he used until it fell apart from too much wear. The bird was always the same when it fell, so torn and interrupted that it broke your heart just to look. But so sensational, the movement of the bird and the man together, that once done it was never forgotten and was always as good in the act as in the anticipation. Reardon looked up as the colonel, a duck in each hand, came striding toward him, a huge grin on his face.

"You missed two," he laughed.

"What do you expect with this popgun?" Reardon was grinning.

"Americans are wonderful with excuses," he said.

"Shit," Reardon said. "My God, those birds are fast."

"Tough," he said, hefting his two, his thick fingers in a V under the ducks' heads.

"It's great shooting. God, it is wonderful shooting."

"Better than North America?"

"Damn right," Reardon said.

They began the slow climb back to the camp, hampered now by the heavy birds and the guns. They climbed swiftly, leaving the pond behind them, hearing only faintly now the cries of the blacks as they moved back to the water. Reardon had to halt once, to catch his breath in the thin air. The colonel waited patiently, then they resumed the climb to the top of the rise.

So they plunged back into it after a black duck breakfast. They liked each other now, and understood each other better, both exhilarated from the shoot, the sight of the birds, and the cold of early morning. Reardon talked a little of the places in North America where he had shot, the wonderful rich neck of land in the Chesapeake where he went as a child with his father, where the geese and the swan set up a honking like the baying of dogs. But none of the places was as wild as the pond, or the birds as innocent. In the United States, there were licenses and limits and too many people. When his father first began to shoot, there were none of these. The limits came with the people, and with the reduction of game. Everyone cheated a little, by sugaring the water with corn or by taking two limits a day, one in the morning and one in the afternoon. Everyone worried about the wardens. His father's friends did it; he did it; everyone did it. Except for the old man, who quit when they made the rules, quit gunning altogether. In the Chesapeake Bay, a blind rented for five hundred dollars an eight-week season, and it was not even a blind in the water but a trench dug in the middle of a cornfield; and the Indians couldn't afford it, Reardon said with a smile. Everyone else became a small-time chiseler. There were rules to the chiseling, such as how much sugar was reasonable and fair, and most thought that to bait the water blinds was wrong. Wardens came over the land in light aircraft, looking at the gunners through binoculars. It became a game to outwit the wardens without spoiling your own sense of what was right, what made good sport; the state's rules were intolerable, so you made your own, and tried to stick to them. But the gunners knew they were chiseling.

The colonel asked what a limit was, and who the wardens were. Reardon explained, and the colonel nodded. He said that when life became more tranquil he would buy himself a repeating shotgun, a pump Winchester, to make doubles and triples without reloading. When he was in the army, officers returned from tours in the United States with repeaters. Well, he thought he might arrange for a Winchester anyway, even before life became tranquil. One had to eat.

"Keep the game wardens away after the revolution," Reardon said.

"No tax collectors or game wardens."

"And issue no visas."

"No foreigners," the colonel said, pouring again from the brandy bottle and smiling.

"No one comes in, no one goes out."

"Yes."

"Of, by, and for Indians."

"And Winchesters for everyone."

"Well, make your own Winchesters," Reardon said. If this country was going to be utopia, it might as well be a real utopia.

"No foreign goods?"

"Right."

"If you say so, Reardon."

"No *machinery*, Colonel."

"We will make our own."

"The first nail in the coffin of the revolution."

"You don't know Indian machinery, señor."

The diversion ended after breakfast. The colonel was a man of a single track, and while he might joke with Reardon about Winchester shotguns for awhile, it was necessarily for a very short while; then he came back to the point. He repeated the plan, the method of seizing the radio station; why he needed Reardon there, someone to identify and pull the switches. There was only one thing worse than a lost cause, and that was a pointless one. And if the radio were penetrated, and through lack of knowledge the colonel was unable to broadcast—that was pointless, a calamity; a pointless risk. He was obsessed with the problem and repeated it. He was not a romantic, he said, and wanted not a gesture but an act. *I am not making a gesture, Reardon.*

Reardon knew he was vulnerable and continued to object; his contribution to gesture. But this was not his show, and never could be. Permit me to return to my holy cards, Colonel; we are better fitted for holy cards, and the general price index, the odd irrigation project; sunrise services. They were high-yield, low-risk bonds; blue chips, nothing ventured, something gained. He tried to explain to the colonel how his life was rooted elsewhere, how what he had come from was too complicated to be very satisfactory in the service of a guerrilla. It was not an American show, Reardon said finally and definitely; if you include an American it is a disaster. Reardon left it at that, looking at the other man across the table, wondering what the Indian thought about the timid American, the seminarian radio operator, distributor of holy cards, tranquilizers, a sometime voluptuary, Roman Catholic rainmaker. He didn't have the conscience for it, and tried to tell the colonel that, too. Colonel Robin Hood and the most ill-assorted merry men, the most ill-conceived raid since Napoleon's march into Russia, a plan with the seeds of catastrophe planted everywhere—and now an American in on it.

"I was a monk," Reardon said abruptly.

"So?"

"A *monk,* Colonel. I prayed for four years."

He nodded, and reached again for the brandy bottle.

"I wanted to become a priest."

"And I have got to have a man who knows the radio," he said, pouring brandy carefully into the two glasses. Some of it spilled, and dribbled onto the table.

"Look, Colonel. I have explained about the radio. It is complicated, true. And there is a chance that it would require an adjustment. But there should be no trouble with the diagram, and I can show you how to make the adjustment."

He shook his head. "The risk is too great. It is too great to risk the loss of the guerrilla. I won't allow your refusal. It's settled now."

Reardon supposed that it was. Odd. How strange. He found himself pleading, not for reasons of fear or for reasons of politics, but from some vague sense of the . . . rightness of it. How could there be fear when it was so unequal? Now it was all wrong; and the longer he looked at the heavy man across the table, the worse it got. His eyes drifted from the Indian to the map behind him, and the packs and weapons on the floor under the window.

"It is important that it be done right . . ." Reardon began.

"We will win because there is no other possible outcome, señor." He spoke mechanically, sincerely but mechanically; it was a speech he had given before. "We will win because we are tougher, and because we know what we want. And because there are no regrets. And because we know what we need to do to survive. It cannot be stopped, Reardon. Not with the largest army in the world. The cause is greater than armies. It is as certain as the wind on that plain. I need only one victory to make that wind into a storm. We are going to take the radio, Reardon. And you are with us, like it or not."

He stared across the table suddenly angry, a little drunk, his hands shaking, trying to hold it back and failing, looking at Reardon through his blank eyes, squinted now with fatigue and anger; or more than anger, contempt for a man in the middle.

But the choice had been made. Reardon rose and walked to the door of the hut, and pulled back the canvas covering. It was raining softly after a quick period of sun, and there were more ducks on the pond. The pond was as it had been before, serene and continuous, unruffled. Reardon felt his chin; he needed a shave. He was four days without a razor, and it reminded him of the monastery before the communal electric shaver. The novices shaved once a week with battered razor blades, a twentieth-century hair shirt, which nicked and cut their faces. They patched themselves with tissue. But the electric shaver had ended all that.

Well, the *jefe* needed a shave more than he did. He also needed someone in that radio station. But not an American. It was a personal thing. He really ought to keep away, if he could keep away. It was the business of the guerrilla, of the colonel and Martinez and the rest of them; their fight, not his, and important that they should understand that as well as he. Like the monastery was the business of the monks, Reardon thought; yes, and the thing with the girl in London, that was her business alone. Right. Where was she? Living on the Riviera, lying on the stones of Cannes, listening to music and drinking wine and running a boutique. Boutique? Tell me about boutiques in Acopara: boutiques and astronauts, and the sexual revolution, yes, and the new theater. The Indians would appreciate the theater of cruelty. Yes. If he had stayed in London . . . But he didn't stay in London or anywhere else, so all of this was idle. If he had stayed in the monastery, he would be a priest now. If he were a priest, he could bless the guns, serve communion in the trenches.

What a useful series of thoughts. It was doing him a great deal of good now, standing in an open doorway and looking at a pond full of ducks. He was always very good at thinking. He was thinking about everything except what mattered. But that was out of his hands now, too. If you got into someone else's business, you got what you deserved. Now we are unlucky; the unlucky country. Bullshit. This has nothing to do with the country. Reardon stood alone, feeling his whiskers, looking down at the pond, shivering with cold and dragging his fingers across his chin. He changed the guerrilla by his presence, by the colonel's bringing him into camp; now, by that, a perfect circle, Martinez would use him to fracture the unity. With reason; with a good deal of reason. He was into it whether he wanted to be or not, part of the formula; he was into the equation, and in a different way than the colonel thought. Reardon was very positive around the dinner table at Deshais's apartment and in the reports he sent back to New York, speaking of the church and the government, deriding both, defending (oh, by implication only) the Indians and the rebels, and muttering the little soul-searchers to the padres.

> *We have loved long enough.*
> *Now, finally we wish to hate.*

Ever the careful observer, neutral on one side or the other, admired for dispassion and an instinct for detail; but a man (everyone said so) who knew where the right lay, a man who at some distant rendezvous could be counted on, probably. Now it was his turn. It was not difficult to do the other, and stick with money and concern; high-yield, low-risk efforts. Stay with one job, the one you were hired to do; stay nerveless, run the distance alone. No, señor. Not difficult. Under the circumstances, impossible.

He knew precisely what the guerrilla was up against, what it must do and how; and the odds. He had come a long way and now he was sitting with a middle-aged man who dreamed of a revolution, who thought that if he spoke people would follow, because he spoke as a part of them. We will win because there is no other possible outcome, he'd said; because we know what we want. There was no manifesto, only unity.

—Tell me, how did you seize the radio station?

—Unity.

—Unity won it?

—Right. We rolled unity up to the front door, and put a shot over the tower. A whiff of unity and the radio station was ours. The enemy surrendered, and the people rose up as one, cast off their yokes, and were free.

—Amazing.

Reardon looked away from the pond. Where were the men, the ones who would shortly begin a revolution? They were rough-housing near the makeshift corral, playful as cats, cuffing each other and falling down, laughing and rising again to join battle. Their guns were laid to one side, a haphazard pile of thick sticks. There were no sentries, no one watching any of the approaches. Two in the middle were preparing to arm-wrestle. They stretched out full length in the dirt, the sleeves of their shirts rolled up to the shoulder. The others gathered in silence to watch, squatting on the ground and chattering, up close to the contestants. Fifty yards away, Reardon felt the tension and energy. One of the wrestlers was the boy, Hernan. The two set themselves, arms up like railroad semaphore signals, eyes locked on each other. They began, each shuddering from the force, their necks arching and their eyes moving down. Hernan quickly worked his opponent's hand almost to the ground, the veins in the other's hand almost touching the earth, his own face red and shaking with exertion, his left arm stiff at his side, then gripping his thigh for leverage. He had done it in five seconds, and now smiled painfully, gather-

ing for the *coup de grâce*. But nothing happened. The other permitted his hand to rest half an inch from the ground, all of Hernan's
strength in his palm now; but he could not force it down. Then
with a thin smile his opponent began the counterattack. He stared
straight at the boy first with a smile, then with fierce concentration, then relentlessly, smoothly as an oiled machine, his hand and
arm moved from the ground in an arc. The boy began to shake as
he tried to hold, his feet grabbing for a purchase on the earth, his
head down and his lips working. But the other would not be
stopped. His hand went up and over in an arc, steady and strong
as a shadow from the rising sun. Still grinning, he held the boy's
hand a fraction of an inch from the dirt. Reardon knew that it was
over when the others gave a shout, and commenced to pummel
the boy, who sat upright rubbing his arm, his hand shaking like a
butterfly. The winner was grinning and driving his right fist into
his palm, flexing fingers to show that he wasn't tired, that he
could do it again now, against all comers, against anyone; that he
had been playing, that he had permitted the boy almost to win,
then took it away from him. Another of the men got down on the
ground, and Reardon turned away and looked back to the pond.

It was some outfit, the soldiers arm-wrestling while the commander plotted the violent overthrow of the government. Twelve
men and their horses, six Stens and six shotguns and a Browning
automatic rifle. And a record of survival. And the wholeness of
the plain, and the people on it. There were shouts now from the
men, and Reardon knew that the winner was winner and still
champion. The commotion continued. Where was Martinez?
Martinez and the others would follow now, but they would not
follow forever. They would not follow for the same reasons that a
son does not follow a father. The colonel, Pacheco, was a different

breed altogether. Martinez and the others would never have taken an American into camp, not to seek his advice or because they needed him or for any other reason; they would as soon have confided in the major commanding the garrison, or in the minister of interior, or in the chief of the civil guard. But the colonel did. The colonel did because he wanted the radio; he was willing to suborn everything to the radio. Purity came after success, acts before gestures; and of course he had all that unity.

Reardon looked back at the men and out over the pond and shook his head. The ducks were still there, the water now royal purple fringed by white rocks. The light cast softer shadows, and the edges confused and became softer. He rocked on his heels with fatigue, massaged his back, and put his arms over his face to ward off the wind. He had managed to avoid a lot in his life, but he could not avoid this.

Reardon turned and walked back into the hut and nodded at the colonel. He didn't know what made him change his mind, if indeed he had changed it, and probably would never know. He could invent a reason later. Well, it was not a blue chip. Jesus Christ knew it was not a blue chip. He looked at the colonel and said he would do it, do whatever it was that the colonel wanted him to do. It didn't matter whether the mission was a success; well, it wouldn't be. There was no chance, not with these men and these arms, and that plan, and now him. It was counting on the garrison to be even more cowardly and stupid than they normally were; it was counting on heroic stupidity from the major commanding.

Reardon re-drew the map of Acopara, making the distances correct, drawing the inside of the radio station from memory, but drawing it accurately. He wanted the colonel to understand where the switches were, where each switch was and what it did, what had to happen before the radio would transmit. The map of the town and its surroundings was simple. There was a single difficult spot at the point the trail hit the base of the mountain and gave onto a quarter-mile open stretch to a small bridge, and another mile beyond the bridge to the outskirts of the town. It was a bridge where there might be an army patrol, or at the least a lookout. It was the first bad point, and the one where the proportions had to be exact, even though (perhaps because) the guerrilla knew the terrain. The colonel was fascinated with the diagram of the radio station.

They slept from noon until dusk, then arose, and the colonel assembled the men. As Reardon looked on in silence from the rear of the hut, the colonel outlined the plan, speaking very slowly and carefully. He gave them each bit and small point, inviting discussion and disagreement. The men were in a circle on the floor of the hut, inspecting the map and following the colonel's finger as it moved from the camp to the town and back again, marking this point of rest, that of danger. There were two routes, both dangerous. It was very detailed, and not until the end was there serious disagreement.

Martinez wanted to know about Reardon. The colonel took the question and patiently explained about Reardon: he had rendered valuable advice and would render more. The guerrilla did not need him, but he was helpful with the transmitter; he would not be a burden on the trail, and he was vital with the switches. The colonel smiled and said that Reardon's heart was with the revolution; but in case his heart should falter, there were other reasons as well. No one need worry about the gringo. But the men were suspicious, and Reardon didn't like it; he expected it and understood it, but he didn't like it. The men found Reardon an unexpected element at the last minute, a new and inexperienced man whose loyalty was unknown; and a gringo. Martinez was more direct: he told the colonel that an enemy was now with the guerrilla, and what reason for that? This was not the understanding when he had been taken from Acopara.

Brusquely, *Jefe* cut off the talk. Reardon, he said, would go with him. The colonel said he would assemble the plan of attack in consultation with Martinez, and they would be ready to break camp in twenty-four hours, packs checked, weapons cleaned, scouts out. The camp was to be abandoned, all that could be carried taken, and the rest destroyed. The success of the guerrilla was assured, the colonel told his men. But the men did not look convinced.

Chapter Six

REARDON WAITED while the colonel talked with his men, checked the weapons and the food, verified that each man knew the route in case of separation. There were only two maps, one for the colonel and one for Martinez; the men would rely on memory if the parties became lost. The mood was tight and buttoned up, as the guerrilla made its final preparations.

A runner that morning told them that army patrols were scattered around Acopara, asking questions of the people and roughing up an old man in the process; they were being rougher than they needed to be, and the town was alive with talk. There were rumors growing from Reardon's disappearance, and the rumors expanded with each new meeting between the priests and the major at the garrison. The old priest, Deshais, made one visit three days ago and two visits a day later; he appealed from the pulpit for information. The police and the army were in and out of the church, questioning those who worked there. Of the rumors, the one the colonel preferred was the story that Reardon had gone with a woman, taking the collection plate with him; the woman had spirited him out of town, and now they were in North America, in New York or Los Angeles, living well and out of the heights and cold of Acopara.

The runner was filled to overflowing with information. He said that the army was patrolling with its customary caution. It moved in platoon rank, forty men, some on horseback, some on foot. There was no attempt at concealment, and there were only three patrols a day, two to the northeast and one to the northwest, nothing at night. There was one report that a squadron of aircraft had been sent from the base near the capital, and two planes were seen loitering over the town. The colonel told Reardon that at best the runner's information was half false, a mixture of natural Indian pessimism with a desire to appear fully informed; it was information to be taken seriously, but not entirely seriously. The job was to winnow the good from the bad.

The colonel liked the part about the squadron of aircraft, American jets with air-to-ground missiles slung under their wings, .50 calibre cannon in the nose; one-million-dollar, 600-mile-an-hour machines that idled slowly and lethally. And uselessly, the colonel laughed; useless as hell. Armies were the same the world around. If there were a body of water anywhere nearby, the navy would have sent frigates; if it had any frigates. As it was, it had admirals; very well then, it would send admirals. They all wanted in on the kill, if there was any kill. The colonel had been an army man, up through the ranks, and knew how it worked. It was a chain of command from the joint general staff in the capital to corps and region and finally to a major at a garrison on the edge of Acopara commanding two battalions of troops and an artillery battery. Word came that a North American was missing; perhaps there was other intelligence as well. At the garrison, the commander saw a target of opportunity: to distinguish himself, to get men into the field, to maneuver. His officers were bored, his men out of condition. It was a fine garrison, but it had to fight to keep its trim. Get them out of the garrison and into the field—not all of them, because the garrison was itself vulnerable, but three platoons, four perhaps. The element of the missing gringo was yet another opportunity for senior officers at joint staff. They would invite the American military attaché to watch the exercise. There was a factor of risk, but it was not great if the attaché were kept aloft, permitted to watch the maneuvers from an airplane. It could be an on-the-spot demonstration to the Americans that the situation was well under control, contained certainly, *but that danger existed.*

The colonel shook his head, laughing and confident that he knew his enemy's ropes. It was crazy. Instead of sending two dozen patrols, of six men each, far out to find a trail, they sent three patrols of forty men each, elephants chasing rabbits. They sent their aircraft up, they made noise all over town, and the people understood that something was happening. They understood that things are not as they were. And that is all the guerrilla needs. All it needs is the understanding that matters have slipped. Something has come loose, out of control. Something has happened that has obliged the government to open the garrison and send large patrols into the countryside; large patrols, not small ones. And aircraft from the capital, and consultations at the church. So what does the population think?

"Put yourself in the place of the population, Reardon," the colonel said. "The population does not think of twelve men in a cave, half-armed with old Sten guns and half-armed with shotguns. It thinks of a rival army, battalions. It thinks of Ché or Fidel. It thinks of the guerrilla across the border, which has met the regular army and defeated it where it has met it. The people think that out there on the plain something is massing; the Indians massing; they are not certain what it is, only that there is *something of consequence.* Not twelve men in a cave, Reardon, with old guns and sickness and low morale and doubtful support and a leader who has been forced to borrow an American to break into a radio station. No. They think of twelve hundred men in rank, with artillery and a colonel commanding, modern weapons and a plan for a general uprising. A method, señor. A method."

The colonel, eyes burning, a hard smile on Reardon, turned back to the map. He seemed taller, straighter, a general balanced on the balls of his feet, smoothing a nonexistent tunic. He was the product of West Point or St. Cyr now, familiar with Austerlitz and the Peninsular Campaign and Dien Bien Phu, blooded in battle himself; slapping a swagger stick against his thigh, confident. There was an army at his command: one command and an army would obey. The essence of leadership, command, and obedience. But it passed very quickly, the shadow, and the colonel turned back to his audience of one.

"It may be a single one-day alert, although the squadron does not sound like a simple one-day affair to me. The air force has shortages of gasoline; the president of the republic does not send a squadron after a missing gringo, not on the word of a major in charge of two battalions. Word comes from higher than that. It is possible they know more than merely the fact that a North American is missing, although that may be reason enough. It is true that there are bandits; the gringo might have gotten lost, wandered away. It could be an excuse for maneuvers . . ." He looked at Reardon, wanting confirmation.

"Possibly," Reardon said.

"But not likely."

"No," Reardon said. "Not likely."

"It is difficult to tell about the patrols. They are afraid to send out small ones, afraid the men will defect. So they are forced to send large ones, with a lieutenant in charge. The is the trouble with a conscripted army. No discipline."

"Unlike the guerrilla," Reardon said.

"Correct," said the colonel.

Bending over the maps they worried it together. When did the army discover it, whatever it was that provoked them to put patrols into the field? The first day? The second day? Perhaps it was a combination of a missing gringo and other intelligence. They would surely trace Reardon to the café, and the five men at the table. Perhaps the owner would recognize Martinez. Perhaps he heard the conversation, the talk of a long trip on horseback. Thank God Reardon had not mentioned the Indian in the alley. But it was a safe café, and the owner would give away nothing voluntarily, even assuming he had something to give. But if they beat him . . . No, there could have been no leaks nor treachery. Who was there to pass information? No one knew anything except the colonel and he made his plans as he went along, improvised one day to the next, never entirely certain of the objective or the destination, or the route to the destination. Plans revealed themselves as they proceeded, sometimes under control, sometimes not. There was no date set for the radio station. The routes of approach were not set. And for what purpose could they imagine the guerrilla would need a gringo? A hostage? A kidnap? Unlikely, and as time passed with no ransom note, increasingly unlikely (and if there was a ransom, who would pay it?). The gringo knew about irrigation and about the radio station. He knew about the radio station and was different from the others, stood outside the mission. Well, it would not be difficult to deduce, even for a major.

But nothing was set in concrete. The colonel planned everything himself, occasionally calling in Martinez. And Martinez had not been called in on this in a serious way. It was one cause of his nervousness and his anger, his dark face. But it was the only way to work, until the guerrilla was functioning smoothly, with confidence; until the successes came, and a structure could replace one man. Then there would be other leaders. But now there was only one, and that was the way it should be. No, treachery from the inside was impossible.

The colonel examined the thought, turned it around, rubbing his hands through his thick hair, looking at the map and worrying some more, tapping the desk top with his finger. Finally he spoke out loud to Reardon.

"They may understand about you back at the garrison. They may know we have taken you and why."

"I don't think so, Colonel. My connection with the radio is slight. There are others who know more about it than I. There are better men to kidnap than me."

"Who? Father Deshais? What is the name of that other one, Francis?"

"Not Deshais," Reardon said. "But Francis knows about it. The Indians who work there know about it. It is not logical to take an American, Colonel. It doesn't make sense." As if anything did. He thought that there was no use the two of them worrying.

"Perhaps not," he said, shaking his head and moving now

around the room, distracted. He checked the gear, peering into the packs against the wall. Each man had food for five days, and ammunition, and a poncho for the cold, and a sleeping blanket. Martinez would take one compass and half the medical supplies, the colonel the other half. The medical supplies amounted to bandages and morphine. Martinez was a competent medic, but the colonel knew nothing about it; knew nothing and cared less, understood only to put a white bandage on a wound and adminis-ter morphine when there was shock or pain. He was personally looking at the packs, and then called for the men outside.

They were waiting in front of the hut and now came in through the door, Martinez first, and grouped around the table. The colonel went to each man, wishing luck, clamping one hand on the shoulder and the back, smiling. He took each weapon and inspected it, talking as he tested the clips and the triggers. The men were excited and quiet and the tension began now. Martinez stood on the outside of the group, watching the colonel go to each man, speak of the importance of the mission, and pass on. The colonel finished with all of them, walked over to Reardon and handed him a Sten. Reardon accepted it with a smile, and slung it on his shoulder. Then they got down to business.

He reviewed the mechanics of the radio, what he would do and what the colonel must do if there was a slip. He spread the di-agram in front of them and carefully explained how to activate the transmitter. There were four switches, and he drew small pic-tures of all four. When the transmitter was activated, a red light would shine from the center of the control board. When the red light appeared, there was one other switch to pull. When the colonel spoke, a needle would register his voice; Reardon, at the controls, would keep the needle below the red mark on the dial.

Reardon explained to the colonel the importance of modulation, and clear diction. He warned him that a man could sound like a fool over the radio; the voice must be kept low and modulated, words never slurred.

The colonel stared at him, puzzled.

"Sell the revolution like we sell beer, Colonel."

"What?"

"Rhyme it and set it to music."

"I do not understand," he said.

"It is an important revolution. Speak about it importantly. The consumers will not believe you unless your voice has a certain tone and . . . authority."

"Reardon, what are you talking about?" the colonel asked, impatient and anxious to proceed.

"The latest techniques, Colonel."

"Keep them to yourself."

"What I mean is, keep your voice low. Speak softly and very clearly."

"Yes, yes."

The men came close to the table, bellied up to it, and the colonel told them that Reardon would explain the terrain of the radio station, and what they were likely to find there. Reardon spoke in Spanish, slowly, and the colonel translated into the dialect.

"It will be a simple matter to get inside," Reardon said. "They are conventional padlocks (he drew them), and there is a chance they will not even be secured. In any case, I have a key; and if the key is lost, they are simple enough to break. You enter an auditorium (make very certain there is no one in it; Indian children like to come in to sleep at night) and go through the door to the right of the large windows. That will bring you to a room which holds the recordings. Go through it and into the large studio. It is the studio from which the colonel will broadcast. I will go to the control room. There are two guards, both unarmed, both of whom usually sleep."

Reardon looked up. All of the men were peering intently at the diagram.

"The two guards are *here* (Reardon indicated a spot on the diagram) and *here*. One will surely be in the large studio. Both are old men, and do not expect trouble. They are supposed to be near the front door and the rear, but almost certainly they will be sleeping. The large studio is *here* (tapping the diagram). Once again, you must position men *here* (pointing again) and *here*. Outside, the station can be reached from only two streets. You must have one of them for your withdrawal . . . "

"I know the withdrawal," the colonel said.

". . . is down the street, and out the alley. You pass the café. Avoid the plaza and the church. It is well-lit, as you know. And often there is a policeman near the church, and sometimes in it. So don't go through the plaza. Go around the other way. Clear?"

"I know the withdrawal, Reardon. Tell me about the radio station."

Hunched over the diagram, very serious now, Reardon did not look up or appear to have heard the other, speaking at his elbow. "There are only two ways they can attack once you are in the station. They must come down one of these two streets (he indicated them). There is no other way. Men at the top of these streets can keep them down, keep them back. If the troops are as badly trained and as cowardly as you think they are (he glanced up at the colonel, standing impassively, listening carefully, and translating), it should be no difficulty to keep them off. With any luck it should be simple to join again, once the broadcast is made. There is need for only two men with Stens at the top of each street. You should give one of them the Browning, Colonel. A Sten can control all the approaches. There is no need for accuracy, only fire; only lead, and a lot of it. At a signal from you . . ."

"I know the town, señor."

". . . they withdraw, firing as they go. Then you move up the alley and out the way you came. As you have said, Colonel, if there is a lot of shooting before the broadcast is made, then it is pointless. Afterwards, it will be very difficult to get away out of the town. It is best to have no shooting, no?"

"Tell me about the radio station."

"The point is this: it is almost windowless. Only two windows on the street, and those have bars. The problem will be in getting the transmitter to work, but I will deal with that. If you attack at five, then broadcast for ten minutes, maybe twelve, you should be out of the station by half after five, before the regular crew arrives for work. It is entirely possible that no one at all will interrupt you. The garrison is not awake then, only the countryside. If someone is listening, it will take time to bring the army to the station. It is possible you will get away with no shots being fired at all. As you have said, Colonel, the point is to do it silently . . ."

"You are too hopeful."

". . . because shots will surely bring the police. After the police, the garrison, and then you are fighting a battalion, and maybe the air force. Do it all very quietly, Colonel. They do nothing in that town at night except sleep and drink. Only in the countryside are the people awake, with their radios turned on, waiting for the morning music from Acopara. Those are the important ones."

"You draw a good plan, Reardon."

"I want to see you succeed, Colonel."

The men stood silently for a moment, looking at the diagram. Then Martinez spoke. He ignored Reardon, and asked his questions of the colonel. What if there were not two guards, but four? What if the locks had been changed? Why was it that the switches were so complicated? They did not seem complicated to him. What if the army had surrounded the radio station after the gringo's disappearance? The colonel answered the questions, then went on to explain that the guerrilla would break into two at dusk, in an hour's time. Both groups would leave at dusk, fifteen minutes apart, with instructions to rendezvous at midnight of the fourth night. Each would know the other's approximate position at all times, and was to maintain maximum alert. Martinez was in charge of the second group. Sullen, bad-tempered, he again warned the colonel that none of the signs was favorable: a full moon the night of the attack, and the feeling (he did not describe it) of great danger. Martinez spoke so quietly he was barely audible, and the colonel ignored him. He had a final exhortation.

The guerrilla would seize the radio station and bring revolution to the lives of the people, inform them that a movement was here, and that it belonged to them, that the government would fall and the people would benefit. Not prosper, *benefit*. The foreigners and the bloodsuckers would be thrown out. The landlords would go, and the petty officials along with them. The army was weak and its commanders cowardly. The land belonged to the people as the country belonged to the people; the country was corrupted by those who led it. The guerrilla would return what was theirs to the people. It was necessary to fight in order to prevail, and to prevail in order to survive.

Martinez began his complaints in earnest after that. The arms were light and inaccurate. Two of his men were ill, one with diarrhea and the other with cold sickness. "I am uncertain of the route, even with the map and the explanations. The horses are neither well-fed nor strong. Much can go wrong. Much now is open to chance. The guerrilla strikes only when certain of victory."

"So you want to quit?" the colonel said softly.

"No."

"Tell me the other plans, the other courses of action."

Martinez was silent.

"An assault on the garrison, perhaps? The administration building? Perhaps a pueblo?"

Martinez shook his head.

"There are none, comrade. This is it. This is the only plan we have."

Martinez spoke in a low whine, the colonel answering him slowly but clearly and definitely. Martinez now stood apart from the other men, and continued:

"There is the gringo, *Jefe*." The gringo: symbol of the foreigner that the colonel, the entire guerrilla, wanted out of the country. The gringo had no right to be involved in this, to be involved now, with the radio . . . they soiled everything they touched. They were bad omens. Reardon was a bad omen.

"We have all had experiences with the gringos, *Jefe*," Martinez said. He was pleading now. "Let this one go back to Acopara, where he came from. Or North America. Or keep him here until we have finished our business. He is bad luck." Martinez: a young man with an old face dressed in the heavy cloth and wool cap of the Indian, long-legged, lean, eyes black and small as bird's eyes. He was tall for the plain, powerfully built with huge shoulders. His age was twenty-five, but he looked older. He and the *jefe* had spoken often of discipline, and Martinez had never challenged. But he was challenging now.

Nervous and suspicious, resentful finally of the new element of the gringo; he did not understand what the *jefe* was doing. Why? It was the one thing above all the others that they had agreed upon, agreed on absolutely for the last three years. It was what the guerrilla was based on: no outsiders. He wanted the *jefe* to know that he had not forgotten. The *jefe* ought to know what he, Martinez, thought and what he counted on happening, that he didn't forget or change in order to accustom himself to new circumstances. Reardon was a bad omen, worse now with the Sten he had in his fist, a Sten he probably didn't know how to fire, and in a bad spot could not be depended upon to aim the right way. The gringo was a deliberate offense. It was more than a North American face that made Reardon a bad omen. He was representative of the foreigner, and therefore a *pishtaco*.

The others were blank-faced, hiding behind hooded eyes, watching to see how it would be handled. Martinez had taken the Sten off his back and now stood with it awkwardly cradled in his arms. He was looking at Reardon and moving back. The others stood away, watching the colonel, in front of them now, pulling maps from his pockets.

"See these, comrades; and these. These are maps . . . "

"Don't tell me about maps, *Jefe*. Tell me about the foreigner."

"The foreigner stays," the colonel said.

"A foreigner."

"I will take responsibility for the foreigner."

"And all that we have said?"

"All that we have said is true," the colonel said. "But the foreigner is necessary."

The anger that lay in Martinez, knotting his stomach and turning knuckles white around the butt of the Sten, now burst: "It's not good enough. No gringos!"

The colonel took two steps forward and slapped Martinez hard across the face, spun him around dazed. He shuffled up to Martinez and swatted him like a fly, and the younger man went back hard against the wall, still holding the Sten. His eyes were white with hatred, and sweat erupted on his forehead in small drops. He controlled himself, said nothing, looking first at the colonel and then at Reardon; the colonel was up against him, close, looking into his face. Then Martinez dropped his eyes and backed off.

Sten in hand, he moved backwards toward the door. The movement of his arms swung the gun first at Reardon, then at the colonel. He moved back very slowly, looking from one to the other. *Pishtacos* came in all forms, he thought. They were Indian or mestizo or gringo. They lived far away. They were plague, a bad strain, living in the high mountains, bringing malevolence. Now this one was here, and why? Now the gringo was following them out. He looked at the colonel and mumbled: *pishtaco.*

So that was the way it was. There was nothing to be done about it now. The chief was a good fighter, and had proved that, but was erratic. His ideas were erratic. There were very few of them whom you could trust; they had to be absolutely of your own blood. It would be settled later, after the radio. Perhaps they would split, and he would take one group and the *jefe* the other; *Jefe* could operate across the border. But now he wanted nothing to do with the gringo. Let that one stay in town, where he belonged, in the gringo church with the rest of them, reading the lesson for the mestizos. Let him stay there and rob. Now if the maps were wrong, it would be on the gringo's head.

Martinez was looking at them in the silence, then swiftly left the hut. The colonel followed, and Reardon could hear them talking dialect, the voices rising and falling off. Finally they moved out of earshot, and the others left the hut without looking at Reardon. He heard them saddling the horses and checking their weapons again. It was very cold and when the colonel lifted the canvas to come through the opening, a swirl of cold air came in with him. The murmuring and movements of the horses grew faint as Martinez's group left camp and moved off to the southwest.

"He is a good man, although I don't have to make excuses to you," the colonel said.

Reardon nodded. He did not seem a good man at all.

"Very brave, Reardon. I hope you will not have occasion to see how brave."

"*Pishtaco*. You know, he thinks I am a *pishtaco*. Maybe you too, Colonel. Maybe he thinks you are a *pishtaco* too."

"It is all mixed up in his mind. *Pishtacos* are not only Indians but any scavenger"—he said the word in English—"and to him the gringos are scavengers."

"You mean bloodsucker, not scavenger."

"Yes," the colonel said. "Bloodsucker."

"Some difference," Reardon said.

"You are lucky he didn't shoot you. I'll be frank with you: I thought he would. It surprised me he didn't."

Reardon was not surprised at all. So he nodded at the colonel. "The radio was more important," he said.

The colonel seemed about to reply, then didn't. He went to the table and arranged his papers. Everything in the camp had been destroyed or packed and taken elsewhere. He had worked all day on the radio announcement. Very brief, it ran to less than ten minutes. He enjoyed the saying of it, pacing in front of the table, speaking quietly, not dramatically, but saying it very clearly. The words must be heard. The colonel named no names, the movement was the guerrilla, he was *El Jefe*. No promises, no expectations, no rewards, no call for a general uprising, merely a statement of conditions and an affirmation that a rebellion was underway—then minutes of pitiless scorn on a government and army, and faith in the people. Unity. A movement, a method greater even than the ancients. History. Sacrifice. Discipline. Unity. "He considered himself a soldier of this revolution without even worrying about surviving it." The colonel translated from the dialect for Reardon.

It was good, made without dramatics, without bravado, in its sheer confidence a promise that thousands were arming in the countryside, preparing a final blow for the government. Reardon was moved, and almost believed what he heard; it was almost good enough to believe. Pacheco spoke for the masses of the high plain and stayed away from everything else: no fists, no fronts, no solidarity. It was a message given without reference to other heroes or to other struggles. *Us. Our* revolution.

"It is more than propaganda," he said.

"Much more," Reardon agreed. "I hope enough are listening."

"I do not need the nation, Reardon. Just the Indians, and not all of them. Just a few of them, enough to tell others that something is here other than the government, its taxes, guns, and officials. Its shit aircraft. The foreigners. Just a few Indians listening, no more.

"Well, I hope they are there," Reardon said.

So the guerrilla split in two, an uncertain and angry Martinez at the head of one group and a superbly confident colonel at the head of the other. About half in each group had Stens, the rest shotguns; the colonel carried the Browning and its two magazines. The colonel and Reardon and their five left directly after Martinez. Four nights at march, the days asleep; one night in a cave, the others in Indian huts. No one knew, or would tell, where the Indians had gone. "To visit friends," the colonel said obscurely, as if they had gone to the seashore for the weekend. But there was always food in the huts, and fresh water. And the atmosphere was one of welcome.

They passed small settlements, and people gathered to watch them march by, the children pointing excitedly at the guns and the old people silent, nodding, their jaws working at coca, watching the procession, wondering but staying silent. The old people behaved as if they saw nothing, and if someone came to ask them, that is what they would say: we saw nothing. They would be able to say it in honesty, with a solemn face. No, *señores*, no one has passed here; the night has been empty. The guns were a calculated risk, but necessary; necessary for propaganda. At each of the settlements the colonel dismounted, taking care to leave the Browning behind. He went to the youngest men, walking very slowly and casually, offering them cigarettes. And finally, confidentially: How many patrols have there been? Were there any aircraft? Had anyone in the pueblo been to Acopara in the past week? Was there activity at the garrison? What are the rumors?

When the colonel finished, the men turned to him. First they spoke of commonplace things, the weather, the crops. Then, hesitantly: Who was he? Were there others in the mountains? How did he obtain guns? And Pacheco replied that there were others in the mountains, that some of them were at Asilo and others near the great range near the border. Friends supplied them the arms. Soon there would be a signal, and the plain liberated, lands redistributed, the land returned to the people, officials and foreigners expelled. The men nodded blankly, not committing themselves to belief. But they saw with their eyes the men with arms, men clearly bound for Acopara, the district town; the town where the garrison was. But they would wait a little before believing it.

There were very few settlements, some of which the guerrilla skirted. They were places that the colonel did not know, or knew and didn't trust. Once on the third night, as they passed a tiny pueblo, a pueblo hardly more than a few houses, a young man burst from the interior of a hut, running to the colonel, calling to him in dialect. The colonel halted, dismounted, and talked to him while the others waited. The colonel offered the young man a cigarette and the two stood talking for ten minutes; or the young man talked and the colonel listened, nodding and scraping the toe of his shoe on the ground. The boy was close, talking at the colonel's face, moving his hands in sharp, rapid gestures. The colonel passed him the Browning to hold, and he caressed it as he would a pet. He raised it to his shoulder and aimed off in the distance, while the colonel stood and watched. At the end of it they smiled and shook hands and the boy returned to the hut, whose doorway was filled with faces watching the colonel with apprehension and fear. The boy stood apart from the others, waving and shouting, *good-bye, luck*. The colonel waved back and nodded, climbed on his horse slowly and looked over at the boy. He said to

Reardon, I need a thousand more like that one, or maybe only a few hundred.

It was a long descent through blackness and cold as the men followed the tilt of the plain, down one ridge and up another, but the last one always lower. The men rode silently, wrapped as mummies, their heads buried in the ponchos against the wind and the cold. The colonel had taught Reardon how to wrap a poncho, so he had some protection against the wind. There were no jokes now, or tricks with the Stens. The wind pushed across the plain, driven a thousand miles, a steady force irresistible and unbreakable, so steady and hard that even the mountains seemed to bend. Their eyes slits, the men faced the wind as a thousand needles on their skin, a wind that enveloped them as water. They rode on as though submerged, and Reardon thought again that men could not survive on the plain, could not prevail against circumstance. And after a time the wind seemed a part of him, a part of his condition, and he leaned into it, fought it and struggled with it as he would struggle with a man or an animal. Then it was one on one, he and it, he and the horse and the wind, and his face froze up and he tasted wool from the poncho when he bit and kept biting, eyes on the earth, leaning. His mind fastened on the wind, how much of it there was and how strong, unstoppable. They rode into it and only the colonel knew the way, understood one ridge from another, seemed able to calculate the direction, southeast. Southeast to Acopara. He rode ahead and the men followed, Reardon among them, slowly descending on the tundra.

Each dawn, the colonel rode to the nearest rise and swept the plain with his field glasses, the warming sun rising behind him and casting fifty-foot shadows, the sun blood-red in the thin air, for a few moments at dawn transforming the earth and the rocks into an unbelievably lovely landscape, almost soft in the freshness of the brilliant light. The very early morning became a ritual, the colonel returning to the hut and shaking his head, bending and accepting a jar of coffee; no, there was no one. No one watching, no one following. They were alone on the plain. The men prepared sausage and bread, and they sat and ate it in silence. The men were always outside, watching for visitors, for intruders, but there were none. That first night the colonel pronounced himself satisfied, turned over, and went to sleep.

Reardon, awake, lay on his back, hands locked behind his head, and stared at the ceiling. The Sten was beside him and he turned slightly to look at it, that ugly, inefficient little weapon, nine and a half pounds of misfortune, British Sten Mark II. Not as light as the new American weapons, but light enough; four kilos, more or less. The book said it had an accurate range of two hundred yards, but the book was full of crap. It was closer to one hundred yards, and no one who had any sense would bet his life on it. It was a weapon of forty-five separate parts, stamped from metal like cookies from a cutter. It was manufactured during the Second World War to compete with the German submachine gun, an efficient and beautifully tooled weapon, the companion to the Luger. But the Sten cost only five shillings to mass produce, five shillings or something like it; perhaps ten. It was economically very successful. So simple was the construction that Stens were made in every underground factory in Europe during the war. The ammunition was similar to that of the German gun, so there was no need to import bullets; you only had to steal them. Reardon looked at the gun with distaste, and ran his fingers over the apertures on the barrel. The trigger was worn shiny, the brass showing bright as a penny, and there were other wear marks.

How many were produced? Millions, literally millions, and even now they were in Eastern Europe and in the old British colonies, Cyprus and the Sudan and Malaysia; they turned up in the Congo and in the Middle East and in Laos, anywhere there was fighting. God knows where this gun had been—in the hands of a Turk near Kyrenia or an Ibo near Enugu, or anywhere of a dozen places in the hands of men pursuing one cause or another. You could write a history of rebellion in the last twenty years by writing a history of the Sten. But you could only talk of the underfinanced rebellions. No decent rebellion would get underway with a Sten gun. Now this one belonged to a guerrilla on the high plain, patched together, working adequately most of the time, satisfactory. The colonel told him that they cost fifty U.S. dollars a gun. A fifty-dollar cookie. Reardon turned over on his side and picked up the gun and laid it on his chest. It felt heavier than nine pounds, and the metal was cold, chill as a stone. He put the butt into his stomach and snapped out the clip. It held thirty-two rounds of 9 mm. ammunition. But you got a prize if it went ten rounds without a jam.

Reardon carefully put the gun down, then stubbed out his cigarette on the floor of the hut. When he looked up, he saw the colonel staring at him.

"You cannot sleep?"

"Tough to sleep in the daytime, Colonel."

"We have a long ride tonight."

"I'm going to sleep now."

"Don't worry about the Sten. The Sten will work all right."

"Sure," Reardon said.

"We do very well so far."

"Right," Reardon said.

"Keep that Sten close by."

"Good night, Colonel."

They were three nights at steady march, long nights without rest or conversation, eating in quick bites walking along beside the horses. The Sten was heavy on Reardon's back, awkward with the barrel poking his spine, his shoulder sore after a few hours. The colonel withdrew into himself, speaking only when he had an order for his men. There were few orders, except the repeated command to keep silence. His eyes were relentless on the black horizon, and the pace never slowed. They kept away from trails and from most of the houses. As they approached Acopara, they became more careful still. Some huts they scouted, weapons hidden, searching for evidence of an army patrol. The colonel's orders now were blunt, and the men obeyed swiftly and silently. The only rest was during the day, and even then there were no fires permitted. Reardon was quickly stiff and sore and cold, despite the poncho. At night, even with the temperature twenty degrees off, it was warmer because he was moving.

In the middle of the fourth night, the guerrilla joined at the summit of the hill northeast of Acopara. Martinez was already there, his horses tethered and the men squatting close together on the ground. The colonel was in good humor. The wind whipping their clothing, the dozen men and Reardon bunched up close and reviewed the plans. Neither group had seen or heard of an army patrol. That meant that the runner was wrong, or that the patrols had been suspended. No aircraft had been sighted. The colonel and Martinez spoke softly to each other while the men listened.

"You saw no signs of bivouac?"

"None."

"What did the people say?"

"There have not been any soldiers, anywhere on this route.

There are rumors in Acopara, but the old woman who heard them couldn't remember details."

The colonel grunted.

"A trick, perhaps?"

"No, *Jefe*. They have stopped patrolling. Perhaps they never were patrolling."

"We would have heard."

"There would be signs everywhere."

"This is all very good, Juanito, much better than I expected."

"Better than I expected, *Jefe*."

The men smiled as they listened. The tension eased, and came off. The army was no threat, and the runner had been wrong; they had walked across the plain as if it were theirs, no challenge. No patrols, no aircraft. It was difficult to do anything serious with conscripts. The army was in its hole, back in its cage. The colonel and Martinez continued to talk, anticipating what the guerrilla faced now.

The terrain was complicated, in deep shadows now and difficult to distinguish. On three sides the town was ringed by high hills. On the fourth was the flat black plain. The guerrilla approached from the northeast, traversing the highest of the hills in an S from top to foot, crossing the bridge and moving directly into town through the shanties, the *barrios,* and the outskirts. The descent was steep, and the footing treacherous. It was the route Martinez had taken Reardon the first night. For the run from the mountain to the town, they would break into four groups of three men each, no one attracting attention, weapons out of sight. From the base of the mountain the men would move into town in groups of three, and if it went as planned they would never even be challenged. At the summit, the colonel spelled out again the formation once they reached the radio station; Martinez and one man would guard the western approach; Mono and one man would guard the east. The others would remain in positions around the building itself; two in the street, two at the door, and two to accompany the colonel and Reardon inside. There were only two streets, east and west; if the army was waiting, Martinez and Mono were to withdraw immediately, return to the *barriadas* and wait it out. In ten days' time they would meet again at the safe house in Asilo. *There was to be no shooting;* but if it happened by necessity, accuracy was everything. The colonel said it as if the men were carrying sniper's rifles instead of Stens and shotguns.

The men were huddled together, with the colonel in the middle drawing a diagram on the ground. It was the third time they had been through it, and were impatient. The stocks of the guns crunched against the earth, and the men breathed heavily in the cold.

The colonel reviewed it, and added an alternate plan: if they were hit and there were wounded, the wounded men would be taken to a safe house, a hacienda, near Asilo. He described it, and gave its approximate location. At the hacienda, there were medicines. But it was a place that was to be used only in the extremity, not for any reason except to care for wounded. He wanted to make sure the men understood that, and went around the group with raised eyebrows. The men nodded.

"Is all of this clear now?"

The colonel handed a map to Martinez.

"We depart in two groups at the end, if nothing has gone wrong. I cannot stress heavily enough: no shooting unless it is absolutely necessary to save your life . . ." He was standing still and solid as a statue.

The men, nodding again, pulled themselves to their feet, shaking the stiffness from their arms and legs. They slung the weapons on their backs and waited. The colonel took Reardon's arm and brought him away from the group.

"What about you?"

"The church is nearby," Reardon said. "When the broadcast is finished, I go one way and you go another."

The colonel looked at him closely: "It's safe?"

"Sure," Reardon said. But he had misunderstood the colonel's meaning.

"Us. What happens to us?"

Reardon was standing bent, his back to the wind, his fists jammed into his armpits. The sound of the wind was a low moan across the summit of the hill. He had the Sten slung on his back, and he was shaking with cold.

"I'll tell them that I took a five-day hike. Or a ten-day hike. Christ, that is what it has been: ten days." Reardon was improvising. He had not thought of the future, what would happen after the radio. ". . . nine days, I guess. I tell them I was in the countryside for nine days, and then I returned to Acopara. I had a survey to complete for Harris. Simple."

"Will they believe it?"

"No."

"I worry then, señor."

"Don't," Reardon said. He thought of Deshais, hunched over the whisky bottle, listening to the account of the days on the high plain, a ten-day excursion with no advance planning, no word to anyone; and alone, without the jeep, without a horse. And the night Reardon returns, the radio station assaulted by rebels. The story was not a likely one, and it would not get by Deshais. For whatever that mattered. "Don't worry," Reardon said. "You won't come into it. Tell Martinez that."

"The army will question you."

"I am a gringo, Colonel. There are limits." But he felt that his tour on the plain was at an end, "terminated with prejudice," as they liked to say. The army, stupid as it was, would not believe a word of the explanation, and Reardon would leave. The army would request that he pack his bags and be gone. The generals, lacking specific evidence, were unlikely to cause trouble for a gringo, and if they decided to cause trouble, Reardon would claim that he was acting under duress. But they would expel him anyway, an undesirable alien. That was something else to worry about. Reardon did not want to leave the plain, because there was no place else to go.

"You are probably right," the colonel said. Reardon, his face stiff and frozen with cold, smiled and looked at him a long time, and nodded in agreement. Then the colonel walked briskly away to join the others.

They descended the hill on foot, leaving the horses at the summit in the care of one man and his shotgun. If there was trouble, a man on foot could move easier and more quickly than one on horseback, doubly so with the run back up the mountain. The land was friendlier now to Reardon, a familiar terrain, and he recognized points on the trail. It was two hours after midnight, the sky dark and starless and cold, the big milky moon hidden by a cloud bank, the town lit only at the Plaza de Armas and at the railroad station. The steel skeleton of the radio tower was lit at the middle and at the top with red lights, the top of the tower way below them now. There were no lights at all in the building and the town appeared empty.

Every hundred yards they paused and the colonel looked below through his field glasses, moving them minutely over the town and back to the bridge at the base of the hill, then west to the garrison. The garrison was clearly seen as the men moved down, strung out on the trail. It was dark except for a single searchlight which probed the hill to the north. Bounded by high concrete walls with turrets at its four corners, the garrison looked like a large American penitentiary, with its turrets and barred windows and guards with rifles on the wall. Inside there were three long rectangular buildings where the troops slept.

Reardon looked at the garrison through his glasses: there was nothing unusual about it, no activity of any kind; even the compound with the major's office and the armory was dark. He could not see whether the guards were at their posts in the turrets; he supposed that they were. Reardon handed the glasses back to the colonel.

Lips pressed tight against his teeth, the colonel watched the walls very carefully: some night they would take it with a hundred men, take it and hold it and leave with the major as hostage. Capture the major and release him at a pueblo without his uniform, but leaving him his pistol and its polished leather holster, daring him to use it. That was the next raid after this one, and it would be the signal; he would plan it very carefully. They could do it a month from now, after the excitement died down. Died down but not forgotten, the colonel thought; it would be a long time before the radio was forgotten. They would need another fifty men for the garrison, to hit it on two sides and sustain the attack. Two heavy weapons, 50 calibres, on each side should do it. What they needed was a few grenades, not many, and no shotguns. Everyone would be armed with Stens and plenty of ammunition. That garrison does not want to fight. You can't fight with conscripts. Well, perhaps he would have to wait two months, to have enough time to assemble the weapons and get them in order. But it would be the beginning of the end, definitely the beginning of the end for the government. The searchlight raked the hill to the north each night. The major was obsessed with ambush; he told Reardon and the American military attaché that day at the garrison that if he was ever attacked it would come from the hill to the north; mortars first, then automatic weapons, then a full-scale assault. The assault would come without warning, and he would defend the garrison as nineteenth-century Italian noblemen defended their castles. He complained to Reardon that the problem with the garrison was that it had no moat. With a moat it would be absolutely safe and impregnable, a fortress. The major considered the idea of placing patrols on the hill, but rejected it as useless and wasteful. A guerrilla attacked without warning, moved silently and fore-armed. He gave the guerrilla great credit for stealth; *stealth*, he called it. An army cannot move or defend itself in stealth, as a guerrilla can. That was why he needed the moat. Reardon told the story the night before, and the colonel laughed in appreciation. It was the mentality of the regular army. The guerrilla had great credit whether he deserved it or not. It was one of the advantages of weakness.

The colonel had the glasses on the rock, holding them steady, feeling the grit of the stone on his chin. Reardon was next to him, leaning into the rock, straining his eyes at the garrison and the land around it.

"Nothing there, Reardon."

"No movement."

"No lights."

"It is dark as hell, *Jefe.*"

"Asleep. I think they are asleep."

They spoke in low voices in the darkness, looking all the while at the dark shapes below them. The colonel glanced up the trail at the men, who squatted each time they stopped. The men blended into the rocks, and were difficult to recognize. Now they were only a hundred yards from the bottom.

The trail was narrow at the base of the hill, space for two men only. It passed through a narrow defile between two boulders, then came straight for the bridge. The plain was all around them. It was a bad, murderous passage with no cover and an open stretch for two hundred and fifty yards. If guards were placed on the river banks, they could watch the approach and not be seen themselves. The river was low and fast-running, now six feet below its banks, but still deep. The approach was tricky and the colonel was taking his time at the base, scanning the bridge and the river banks with his glasses. The light was deceptive, and he stopped frequently to inspect a shadow. The bridge was straight on from where he crouched. The river came from the mountain which curled around toward the town, a half-mile away at the point the river spilled and straightened and ran flat. He was look-ing for signs of horses, or anything moving on the banks or below them, or on the bridge or beyond it. A glint of steel or any sound would have sent them all up the hill. But it was quiet and he put the glasses into the case and closed it with a click.

The colonel had come down alone, to get as close as he could with the glasses. Clouds covered the moon, but the sky was bright enough to see by; he could see what he needed to. The colonel thought that if they got by the bridge they were all right; anything in the town could be handled. He stared at the river again, then scrambled back a hundred feet where the cover was perfect, and large boulders protected the path. He moved awkwardly, the glasses bouncing on his chest, carrying the heavy Browning as though it were a toothpick. The men were strung up the trail five yards apart, keeping silence. The colonel, Martinez, Mono, and Reardon were in the lead, downtrail. All the men had their weapons unslung and were standing at rest, gazing over the tops of the rocks to look at the bridge and the run up to it.

"I don't like it," Martinez said.

"No difficulty if no one is there, comrade," the colonel said, whispering it into his ear, bringing his face up tight with the other's, his gritty voice traveling no more than a few inches. "And it is the only approach we have. It is unavoidable."

"No cover," Martinez said.

"I know it," said the colonel slowly. This one wasn't like any of the others. The guerrilla had become an expert in ambush, which was an encounter at one's own place, at a time of one's own choosing. One man could control it from the beginning to the end. If the fish took the bait, that was all there was to it, if everyone did what he was told. It was very simple. But this was different because the colonel did not know what was at the bridge; he thought he knew but he couldn't be sure. And he only had twelve men.

He decided then not to risk a direct approach. He had in mind sending Martinez and three men first, and when they reached the banks to scout, and signal the others. It was the quickest way. It would be Christ-awful to get hit here, on the hill; it was nearly impossible to get back up to the top, and vulnerable once up it. The bad alternatives came to his mind one by one, in rank, and he considered each in turn. They had done well so far. The descent was accomplished in silence, each man ten feet from the other, everything buttoned up and watchful. It was very professional, the men for the first time behaving with discipline and care. But the colonel was worrying now. He handed the glasses to Reardon before sending Martinez across.

The terrain told Reardon nothing. Tensed, he shifted the Sten while he looked through the glasses. *There,* nothing; to the left and right, nothing; along the banks, nothing. No movement of any kind.

"Ah, señor—if only I could count on their sleeping. If they are there, I think they are asleep."

"It depends on what suspicions they have," Reardon said.

"Suspicions—we all have suspicions."

"I don't like it, *Jefe,*" Martinez said.

Mono squeezed in among them, and he looked with the others. "There is no reason for a patrol to guard that bridge," he said flatly, and went back to the others.

"Mono seems sure enough of it," Reardon said.

"Mono doesn't have to cross it," Martinez said.

"I think we will send one man, not three," the colonel said, softly, almost to himself. "Mono is right: the bridge has never been guarded before. Why now? So one man goes—goes around the side of the mountain and crawls to the river bank *there.*" The colonel pointed two hundred yards upstream, where the river jerked to the south as it came rushing from the mountain, before it narrowed into the deep cut. They could hear the noise of the river, and Reardon looked again through the glasses. There was the water, almost out of sight below the banks, and the metal bridge: old, rusted, a temporary bridge which had become permanent, a bridge for goatherds. And behind it the flat line to the town: no shrub, no boulders, a long flat line to the town and its few lights, the radio station, the church, the railroad. It was an old path, and it ran straight for a mile.

The colonel moved in beside Martinez and explained very carefully what he wanted. Martinez nodded slowly as he listened.

". . . move first along the hill, then cut into the stream. I want you to meet that stream two hundred yards from the bridge, then float up to it. Or go along the banks if there is footing. I do not like the looks of that bridge now, but I cannot explain why . . ."

"Nor I, *Jefe* . . ."

". . . but approach the banks of the stream on your belly. Be very watchful, comrade. If they should hit us here, it is all up. If the bridge is unoccupied, signal to us and we will follow. If soldiers are there, withdraw unless there are only one or two who can be dealt with silently. But if there is shooting, go right away to the mountain without thought of us." He paused a moment. "You better take Jorge with you."

Martinez looked back at Reardon. Then, expressionless, he crooked a finger at Jorge and the two of them moved off beyond the two boulders at the base of the trail. He had the Sten slung on his back, and gripped its muzzle as he ran. The colonel kept the glasses on him as he ran. The Browning was wedged between two rocks, loaded and ready to fire. It was aimed at the bridge. But now the glasses were on Martinez and Jorge as they broke from the side of the mountain and were visible for a moment, running very low. Then they were out of sight as they crawled the distance to the stream bank, disappeared over the lip, and were gone.

The guerrilla waited, the colonel shifting his back against the rock as he watched through the glasses, traced what he reckoned would be Martinez's route to the bridge. If the water was very low, he would be able to scramble along the banks. Otherwise, he would be forced to float in the freezing mountain water. Warming him would be a problem later. It was impossible to calculate the depth at that distance. But Martinez and Jorge would have to be quick now, because according to the timetable they should be crossing the bridge en route to the town. The colonel was confident as he looked at the lights in the distance. They were a little behind schedule, but that didn't matter. It was a clear run to the town. Martinez should be signaling to them in five minutes. The colonel, still watching through the glasses, thought then that they should have rank in the guerrilla. Then he could promote Martinez to captain, perhaps Mono to lieutenant. It was not a bad idea. It would give a structure, some scheme to the guerrilla. There would be lines of authority. But that was what you didn't want. You didn't want lines of authority because after authority came jealousy, and after jealousy, intrigue. All it would mean was more problems. Martinez knew who he was without being called captain. He did not need that, any more than *Jefe* needed Colonel. Colonel was Reardon's word, anyway. Mono got along well enough without lieutenant. After titles came insignia and then aides de camp and then you were worse than the enemy you were fighting. You were forced to write reports, and check what you did with others. No, the group should stay as it was: small, until there were victories, and then large, but still working in small groups. It would be an army of small groups, each controlling a sector. His group would be the leading group, the group that set the policy and coordinated with the others. It would be worthwhile getting out of caves, living like men instead of animals. But small always. You did not need rank for that. The colonel was turning to Reardon to tell him to watch closely, when suddenly there was blood on his face. The rock was exploding in front of his eyes.

Fragments struck Mono, standing behind the colonel, and took his arm off at the shoulder. He dropped as though dead, a bewildered expression on his face, and with an awful gasp that the others only half heard. It was a rifle grenade, fired from somewhere near the bridge, somewhere below them. In panic, the others turned to scramble up the hill. But the colonel stopped it with a shout, and turned back to the Browning and put the glasses to his eyes.

The others went flat, and Reardon dropped and leaned over Mono; his lips were moving, and blood leaked from his shoulder, running down the poncho and gathering in a puddle. The force and heat of the blow had partly cauterized the wound. Reardon made a bandage of his poncho, and tried to wrap it around Mono's shoulder; but it was bulky, and slipped and kept slipping. There was more blood now, pumping from the shoulder, open and gaping where his arm was severed, and from other wounds on his chest and neck. Reardon could see Mono's collar bone, white and polished like a piece of china. Reardon had his Sten off his shoulder, and laid it on the ground. Mono was moving his legs, twitching and kicking slightly, the life going out of him.

The colonel fired two rapid bursts at the bridge, then waited, looking at it through his glasses, seeing nothing. Immediately he knew his mistake and closed his eyes for a second. It was like sending up a signal flare, the muzzle flash precisely indicating the position of the guerrilla; the fact of the firing at all indicating defeat. He slowly pulled the gun off the boulder, and looked at Reardon now huddled with Mono. He heaved the gun down to Reardon and told him to watch, and stood up with the binoculars, frantically searching the bridge and the banks of the river. No one knew what had happened to Martinez, whether he was discovered moving upriver, or whether he was safe, flanking the soldiers now at the bridge, or scrambling back up the trail. Now the colonel could see pinpoints of fire, very low on the banks, and he thought he heard the rattle of rifles. But his hearing was shot to pieces by the grenade explosion and his own fire from the Browning. Then there was a flutter overhead, and another, and the colonel knew they were seen; he thought they were firing from the bridge up-stream where Martinez should be. In a rage, he tore the Browning from Reardon's hands, set it on the stone, and pressed the trigger, pumping an enfilade at the bridge, the slugs ricocheting off the old metal in a shower of sparks. The Browning jumped on the stone, nicking it and rattling like machinery, the copper cartridge cases spitting out of it, flying among the rocks. The powder was in their nostrils now, and Reardon was in front of him, yelling at him for Christ's sake to stop it; to cease fire. It was futile, crazy. Tears of rage streaming down his face, the colonel pounded the rock with the big gun and cursed.

He shouted at the men to hold their fire, but the voice loud as it was did not communicate. Keeping their faces below the rocks, six of them fired in the direction of the bridge. Then the colonel yelled again, and the guns went down. The Stens did not reach the river with accuracy anyway, and it would give those below an idea of how many there were, and what arms they had. As if that made any difference now, with all of them blocked up the trail. But at the bridge, they knew there was a machine gun, and a fool shooting it, the colonel thought. An idiot working an automatic against Christ knew how many troops dug in at the bridge and the banks leading up to it and away from it. So now they knew there were Stens as well. The colonel wondered how many were below. It was a platoon at least; at least a platoon, and probably supporting fire in back of it. He deserved to be shot at sunrise. But Christ, they did it well. They blocked an attack from the trail with one grenade, and it was on target. One grenade, and it landed precisely where it should have landed. They could not have known. All of it was luck, dumb fucking luck, luck that should have gone with the guerrilla.

He sat on the ground, back against the rocks and shook. What now? Mono was dead, or almost dead; he looked to his right and stared at Mono's face. Christ. Well, it was all up. The explosion of the grenade could be heard for miles, and the Browning to the next district. The colonel thought that it would only be fifteen minutes before another platoon would be there. Looking carefully at the bridge, still noting the muzzle flashes, he decided then to withdraw. Or the decision was made for him. There were no other choices. He had overestimated; there were no more than twenty at the bridge, but so what? What do you do then? Shoot your way through the twenty and then through the *barrios,* and then make a stand at the church. Make a stand near the altar, perhaps; perhaps those gringo priests would give sanctuary. The colonel sat on the grounds, staring ahead. Twenty at the bridge were enough; Five were. At the bridge the patrol was firing away from the guerrilla, firing close in to the mountain, the direction of Martinez's approach. Probably they thought that was the direction of attack. They must figure that no guerrilla would be stupid enough to send two men against defended positions at the bridge, a platoon dug in and alert and waiting for it. Asleep. Sleep well, comrades. They were waiting for trickery, *stealth.* One of the advantages of weakness. Stealth. But there was no stealth, or trickery either. Just retreat.

There was nothing to do but withdraw. The colonel, still looking down the sight of the Browning, sent the men back up the trail in threes, each at one-minute intervals. He gave the orders very softly, without looking up from the gun. The men had done well, except for the initial panic. None had fired after that, all had instantly dropped below the rocks; waiting command. They had done very well; even Mono had made no noise. It was very accommodating of Mono. But Martinez could not be helped. He was either dead or on his way out, and there was no telling which. But he was probably dead, most likely dead in the first burst of fire. Mono lay where he fell, his eyes beginning to glaze now, staring full and black at the sky. There was blood everywhere, seeping through Reardon's poncho and staining the ground, congealing in the cold. Mono was dying, was almost dead from shock; that, and fright, and loss of blood. His skin acquired the gray shine and polish of the dead.

The colonel marked his wristwatch. The last group was moving up the hill, with a signal to the colonel. He nodded at each one in turn, muttering a few words in dialect. Their shoes scraped the ground as they moved off. There were only he and Reardon now, and the corpse at their feet; and firing below, random shots fluttering overhead with the sound of birds' wings, dying among the rocks. It was all up, the plan exploded to kingdom come: no radio station, no broadcast, no victory, no headline, nothing. The glorious victory of 5 September, three killed, two captured, has come to this: he had taken twelve men down a trail and had got them ambushed, got three killed and the others in danger. It was stupid. He should have understood that the army, that lazy, graft-ridden, stupid army would watch the route from the north. But still, how were they seen? At three in the morning, the bastard ambush was awake and it fired a lucky shot. No, he had not taken the proper precautions. He did not take care as he should have, and the ambush cut him to pieces like a side of meat. Now he would pay for it. God, it was so stupid. Wait another week, two weeks. Wait until it was clear, until it was certain to be clear and the alert off. There was no firing now, but the colonel could see lights coming on in the distance, in the *barrios;* even at a mile away he could see the lamps. What did they think? Perhaps a festival with fireworks at four in the morning. A festival of the Virgin, with roast pig, dancing and brandy; a fiesta. The garrison would be moving, if they had radio communications at the bridge. It would be moving very quickly. Now it was time to leave, and the colonel gripped Reardon by the arm and moved him ahead up the trail. Then he heaved Mono over his shoulder and carrying him like a sack of potatoes followed Reardon. Reardon took the Browning.

Reardon. He had scarcely moved since the rifle grenade hit, and killed Mono. He crouched low behind the boulder and prayed: prayed without direction and without real urgency, but from habit. He lay flat with all the switches off, knowing right away that it meant the end of the mission, and he would go with the colonel. Reardon stopped him firing the Browning, then went flat again to allow others to make the decisions. Once he looked behind him, straight into the eyes of the boy Hernan, the youngest of the guerrilla, a boy who was awkward and untrained and tough, and who had been with the guerrilla since almost the beginning. His eyes were wide with fright, and his legs shaking as if in fever. He looked at Reardon and smiled slightly, an apology. His eyes said, *I am sorry, señor. I cannot do anything with my legs. There they are, shaking like tree branches. Normally they are good enough, but now they are failing me.* The boy gripped his shotgun tightly, and turned his face away, so Reardon looked beyond him, back up the hill away from the firing.

Reardon watched everything come apart, all the ends unravel in misstep. There was no need for any guns, if it was done properly. In and out of the radio station in fifteen minutes, neat and clean. It was so easy, a piece of cake. Infiltrate the town, avoid the police and the army; move silently through the streets, which were deserted before dawn; past the scouts, the electric lights on the corner, enter the station, broadcast and leave. Simple, a lark. But finished now, either by treachery or by dumb bad luck, so now they were lying flat behind a boulder at the bottom of a mountain, Mono dead, and the colonel cursing and watching the bridge through his glasses, the guerrilla in full flight up a mountain that was too steep to climb quickly and, once climbed, vulnerable on a plateau. Everything gone wrong. That grenade landed close, very close; it could have killed three rather than one. Well, that was the luck for today. We lost one here rather than three, or possibly four. Reardon thought that it bounced on the top of the boulder and rolled down, and exploded probably not three feet from Mono. He took the blast. It was a miracle that no others were killed. But Reardon had had nothing to do with it. He looked at Mono and knew now that aid was useless, a waste of morphine; so he said a prayer. He prayed for all of them while he prayed for Mono. Mono was a dead man a second after he looked at his empty shoulder, the shirt in shreds and the blood already starting to spurt. But, thank God, it was not his responsibility. Reardon sat still and waited for the colonel.

But that was over now and the two of them moved back up the hill, keeping low, the colonel grunting and puffing behind him. Reardon shifted the Browning from hand to hand, its fifteen pounds of weight like fifty. More useless baggage, along with Mono. They were a hundred yards up the trail when the explosions came, more rifle grenades hitting off the trail, and low. The ambush below them was lobbing grenades into the trail at random. Reardon and the colonel, still with Mono slung on his shoulder, lay flat for a moment, then knew it was entirely a matter of chance. Their chances were no better or worse to lie flat than to move. The rifle grenades fell indiscriminately, and Reardon suddenly understood what was happening at the bridge. Five, perhaps six, soldiers were standing quietly fitting the grenades into the M–1s and firing them. Two were taking the sector to the left of the trail, and two to the right; the others were firing in the middle, one long, one short. The rifles were not accurate, so it was only an approximation. Perhaps they were talking while they fired, or drinking from a canteen of water.

Below at the bridge there were three men, not four or a dozen or a platoon. They were unable to see the trail, or the men on it scrambling to the top. They argued among themselves where the grenades should go. While they argued, they fired. The shells made a loud POP! as they left the guns and arched toward the mountain, the trajectory of the shell visible at night, the grenades as big as tennis balls leaving the guns and then striking the rocks and exploding. Two soldiers were standing below the lip of the river bank, so that their boots touched the low-running water. The third was looking at the mountain and judging where the grenades ought to go. He told them now a bit to the left, a bit to the right; keep it ahead of them, now twenty yards, now fifty yards. It was all guesswork, although the commands were shouted with authority. How fast are they moving? The men fired with deliberation, calm since the mountain had not returned their fire. The two had four full boxes of grenades, forty-eight grenades, and reinforcements were soon to arrive. After ten minutes with no return fire, the sergeant who had been directing the grenades stood up in full view of the mountain. Smiling, he looked at the trail and tried to remember exactly where it led. He directed the grenades in a wider arc.

The sergeant commanded an excellent defense. The three of them were talking when it happened, and he chanced to look upstream and saw not fifty yards away a man moving along the banks coming toward them. They were below the bridge in the shadows, resting against the metal girders and were not seen. The three rushed to their guns and fired, and the intruder disappeared; perhaps killed, perhaps not. Gone, anyway; fled, and to verify it the sergeant sent the young private upstream to make sure. Then the sergeant personally fired a grenade about a hundred feet up from the base of the trail, where the largest boulders were. And for a moment they thought they were dead, all of them, when an automatic returned the fire and bullets ricocheted off the bridge. They dove for the stream, looking for a route of withdrawal; the young private began to swim. The sergeant hoped the others had not seen his panic; he thought he concealed it, and besides it was no greater panic than either of the others. Perhaps it was not panic at all, just caution. But then the machine gun stopped, and the sergeant after five minutes poked his rifle over the lip of the stream and squeezed off half a dozen rounds. The sound of the gun made him feel better, and he told the others to get out of the water and defend themselves; defend the position. Then there was another burst from the automatic, longer and heavier than the first; the bullets hit the bridge and tore into the banks and the water. For a moment, the sergeant thought the shooting came from upstream; but the private shouted to him that the one there was dead. He thought he saw another moving into the mountains; but he could not be sure.

When the firing stopped, the sergeant moved to the lip; he knew he had to reconnoiter. The enemy would come to the stream from the mountain; Christ, then they would all be killed. He turned to the other private and told him to look over the edge. The other shook his head firmly. No, he would not do that; not now. Later they could look. So the sergeant poked his gun over the lip and fired again, then quickly jumped up. He was up and down in a second, and could see nothing; but he thought that no one was coming from the mountain. There was no answering fire at all, and then he looked over the lip from behind a rock; moved oh so carefully in the darkness and looked out a full minute, concluding that the marauders were moving out, and that they could safely fire back, poke their rifles over first and send them a fusillade of grenades.

The three of them directed thirty seconds of rifle fire first upstream, then downstream. Still, there was no return. They fired at the base of the mountain, first with the rifles then with more grenades. It occurred to the sergeant that the bandits—rebels, whoever they were—intended definitely to withdraw. With his glasses, he saw one figure moving back up the trail. It meant they would not fight. God, he hoped the garrison heard the rifle and sent troops. But meanwhile, he must organize the other two into a proper defense. When the lieutenant came with reinforcements, he wanted him to see how intelligent had been the organization. They would have to have heard the grenades. The rifles and the grenades were making enough noise to wake the dead.

By God, there would be commendations. The sergeant was wild with pride. He tried to wring the water from his trousers but failed. Well, no matter. Crisply, he told the others to station themselves just below the lip, and hold their weapons the way they had been taught at camp. The sergeant stood on the banks of the river and waved his arms, directing the fire higher and higher up the hill.

"You are sure the other one is gone?"

"Certain, sergeant," mumbled the private. He was shaking from the cold and the wet.

"There were two?"

"The other one, an old man, was dead." The private remembered how he had pushed the face of the dead man with his boot.

"It is too bad we didn't kill the other one," said the sergeant. "Well, keep firing."

It was perfection, the sergeant thought. He took no casualties of his own, and thrust back the enemy. It was letter-perfect, the classic defense. He was facing a band perhaps of twenty-five, perhaps of fifty. Doubtless fifty, since they had an automatic gun. The guerrilla. He stood them off with old M–1s and rifle grenades, whose range was short. When the others came, they would come with mortars. The sergeant now undertook the offensive in complete confidence, certain immunity.

There was no fire from the retreating guerrilla because there was no accuracy at that distance, and their positions must remain hidden. Moving low on the trail, Reardon and the colonel, even with Mono and the heavy Browning, made quick time.

"The ambush, Colonel; ducks on a pond."

"Shut up, keep moving."

"Luck! They had luck!"

"Move, Reardon!"

"Luck."

"Move!"

Gasping, stumbling every third step, the colonel was muttering to himself in cadence, cursing those at the bridge who were standing safely and bombarding him with grenades. The dead man was a terrible weight on his shoulder, and finally he was bent almost double, Mono's hand dragging along the ground.

"Five hundred yards!" The colonel thought he had shouted, but the words came out in a whisper, almost a gasp.

"What?" Reardon turned around.

"Out of range! Five hundred yards!"

Breathless, choking from the thin air and the exertion, tasting the sweet taste of copper pennies, the colonel prodded Reardon, kept him moving faster than he thought it possible to move. The explosions were coming off the trail, with crashing *crunch crunch* noises like heavy machinery. The grenades were off the mark fifty yards, but they were sending shards of rock over the trail. They were closer now to the ground, touching the hill and working with it, feeling a part of its mass; they yielded to it, and felt protected by it, their hill. Reardon and the colonel were trotting, or felt as if they were trotting, and ascending faster than the sergeant below reckoned. There was no tree cover, just the trail leading upward, probably two thousand yards more now to the summit; but keeping low, keeping just below the rocks, they were out of sight. Thank God for the dark night, no moon, no stars, only the flashes of the grenades now. His breath coming so short and quick he thought he would suffocate from lack of oxygen, Reardon began to cadence under his breath, *hut hut hut hut hut*. He slapped the rocks on the side of the trail, keeping the measure. He fell once, grabbing onto a rock and tearing his shirt, bruising his legs, the colonel tumbling into him from the rear, head down, dropping Mono and cursing. It was half in Spanish, half in dialect. A long string of Indian words, and then the two of them together: *Hut hut hut hut hut.*

Moving faster than he had ever moved in his life, slipping on the stones, the Browning cradled awkwardly in his arms, Reardon looked only once down the slope, checking the explosions walking toward them. Now there were six or eight men below, and then he heard louder, more violent explosions, and felt the concussion. There were mortars. They knew the trail and they were walking the grenades and mortars up the hill like regiments; there must be half a dozen mortars, and more probably to come. It was almost laughable. There was about to be a slaughter because the three in flight, two alive, one dead, could not move from the trail. The boulders were too big to climb, and they risked being seen. They were running in a tunnel open at the top and all the soldiers below had to do was drop a charge in the tunnel to kill the fish, to stun them or chew them to pieces with shrapnel. God knows what had happened to the others, but they were certainly out of range now, and out of danger; out of range of the mortars and able to move quickly because they were without burdens, without a corpse and a useless machine gun. Reardon was ready to drop the Browning and wheeled around to confront the colonel—but there was no one behind him.

He stood alone for a moment, heaving and blinking his eyes and ducking the concussions. Then he hurried back down the trail. Behind a rock the old man rested, his eyes closed. Reardon dropped the heavy gun and leaned down beside him. He manhandled the corpse off the colonel's shoulders, and rolled it off the trail, blood still seeping from the wound. Reardon slapped the colonel twice, hard, and crazily shook him and gasped obscenities in his face. The colonel's eyes opened and he looked around him in wonder.

"Up! Up you son of a bitch!"

"I . . ."

"Up! Up!"

Reardon bellowed at him, shaking him and slapping his face until the colonel raised his hands to protect himself. But his eyes did not focus. He looked drunkenly around him. Reardon hit him again, hard, and picked up the Browning from the ground. He banged it on the rock, aimed at the bridge and fired. The shell casings flew out of the old gun and clicked against the rocks. He emptied a magazine, the bullets hitting everywhere around the bridge. He thought he saw two soldiers fall, and the rest scramble for the stream. The two who were down sprawled brokenly on the ground. Reardon reached for the other magazine and the colonel looked at him, his eyes dark and hard again. Then he struggled to his feet.

"No!"

"Once more!"

"No! Now we get out."

"Once . . ."

"Out!"

Reardon waved his hand, and pointed at the bridge below them, the water shimmering blackly, the dead men sprawled barely visible on the ground. He was shaking uncontrollably, and forced himself to lean against a rock. He held the Browning against his thigh, the barrel pointed at the earth.

"We save ourselves," the colonel said.

Mono and the gun discarded now, they heaved up the hill on all fours, kicking and puffing like animals. They had to keep to the path, traversing now and climbing one foot for every four they ran. It was very steep and the mortar shells hit above them, sending a shower of shrapnel among the stones. It was dodging raindrops, worse because the rocks were exploding as well. Reardon followed the colonel now, his head thick, his mind slowly blocking off, not focusing, except for a fragment he had read somewhere or heard. It went over again in his mind, a rhythm.

Shrapnel, General Henry (1761–1842). Fought in Flanders, invented the shrapnel shell, filled with shot and a bursting charge.

The colonel was moving away from him, moving faster, and the explosions were closing in. The running room was narrow, and he was not keeping pace.

Used first by the British army at Surinam, then in the something-something campaign, the Peninsular Campaign. Used extensively there-after by all armies. Valuable when precision is unimportant or pointless, a lethally indiscriminate approach to dealing with enemies. One's opponents.

Who else was there? Etienne de Silhouette, Dr. J. I. Guillotine. Those French, well named. But the colonel was ahead and the shells were closer now. He was falling behind again. Where was the Browning? It was a shooting gallery, but there was no direction to the fire. The targets were moving, the explosions walking up the hill, and now shrapnel was everywhere. Exhilarated, Reardon rushed to catch up with the colonel, now a dozen yards ahead of him. He felt his legs buckling, and he told them to go on. Now he was almost at the top of the hill, and once there the horses and the plain, a chance; the plain moved up and away, and there were ridges and valleys under the dark sky. There was protection there. Almost out of range now except that it sounded like more mortars below. The explosions were loud, the last louder than the one before, and Reardon felt the concussions again. He was running and his legs were failing, and he was falling farther behind. But he kept pushing between the rocks, looking for the colonel, now surely over the edge of the hill, safe.

PublicAffairs is a publishing house founded in 1997. It is a tribute to the standards, values, and flair of three persons who have served as mentors to countless reporters, writers, editors, and book people of all kinds, including me.

I.F. STONE, proprietor of *I. F. Stone's Weekly*, combined a commitment to the First Amendment with entrepreneurial zeal and reporting skill and became one of the great independent journalists in American history. At the age of eighty, Izzy published *The Trial of Socrates*, which was a national bestseller. He wrote the book after he taught himself ancient Greek.

BENJAMIN C. BRADLEE was for nearly thirty years the charismatic editorial leader of *The Washington Post*. It was Ben who gave the *Post* the range and courage to pursue such historic issues as Watergate. He supported his reporters with a tenacity that made them fearless and it is no accident that so many became authors of influential, best-selling books.

ROBERT L. BERNSTEIN, the chief executive of Random House for more than a quarter century, guided one of the nation's premier publishing houses. Bob was personally responsible for many books of political dissent and argument that challenged tyranny around the globe. He is also the founder and longtime chair of Human Rights Watch, one of the most respected human rights organizations in the world.

For fifty years, the banner of Public Affairs Press was carried by its owner Morris B. Schnapper, who published Gandhi, Nasser, Toynbee, Truman and about 1,500 other authors. In 1983, Schnapper was described by *The Washington Post* as "a redoubtable gadfly." His legacy will endure in the books to come.

Peter Osnos, *Publisher*